At first glance Red Rock Academy looked like some crappy value inn: a squat, T-shaped, two-story beige stucco building. Except Red Rock was surrounded by a barbed-wire fence and there were two freakishly muscular Neanderthals patrolling the grounds.

"What is this?" I asked Dad, smelling the rat strong now.

"It's just a school I want us to take a look at."

"What for? I'm starting school next week, *my* school, back home."

"That's part of it, sweetheart, you haven't been doing so well back at *your* school."

"A couple of C's. Big deal, Dad. It's not the apocalypse."

Dad rubbed his temples. "It's worse than a couple of C's, and it's not just that. Brit, I've been feeling like you aren't a part of our family anymore. You're not *you* anymore, and I want to get you some help before . . ." he trailed off.

Dad's hands were shaking. The hairs on my arms stood on end. Something was really wrong.

Then the two muscled freaks were on both sides of me, pinning my arms behind my back and pulling me away from the car.

"Dad! Daddy, what's happening? What are they doing?"

"Please, please be gentle with her," Dad was practically begging the goons. Then he looked at me. "Sweetie, it's for your own good."

Sisters in Sanity

GAYLE FORMAN

HARPER TEEN
An Imprint of HarperCollins*Publishers*

HarperTeen is an imprint of HarperCollins Publishers.

Sisters in Sanity
Copyright © 2007 by Gayle Forman

Library of Congress Cataloging-in-Publication Data
Forman, Gayle.
Sisters in sanity / Gayle Forman. — 1st ed.
    p.   cm.
Summary: When a family trip to the Grand Canyon turns out to be a trick
to take her to a remote, all-girl, residential treatment center for unstable
teenagers, sixteen-year-old Brit, devastated by her father's duplicity, comes to
realize that only through inner strength and the help of other inmates who
become her friends can she endure the harsh conditions of the prison-like
institution and plan a way to escape.
    ISBN 978-0-06-088749-0
    [1. Shock incarceration—Fiction. 2. Fathers and daughters—Fiction.
3. Self-confidence—Fiction. 4. Friendship—Fiction. 5. Rock music—Fiction.
6. Coming of age—Fiction.] I. Title.
PZ7.F75876Sis 2007   2007010901
[Fic]—dc22   CIP
                                                                        AC

Typography by Chloë Foglia
09 10 11 12 13   CG/RRDH   10 9 8 7 6 5 4 3 2 1
❖
First paperback edition, 2009

Dedicated to misunderstood girls everywhere

Thank you:
Nina Collins, Maggie Ehrlich, Matthew Elblonk,
Lee Forman, Ruth Forman, Tamara Glenny,
Eliza Griswold, Shahawna Kim, Deanna Kizis,
Kristin Marang, Tamar Schamhart, Nick Tucker,
and Willa Eve Forman Tucker.

Sisters
in Sanity

Chapter 1

It was supposed to be a trip to the Grand Canyon, a trip I didn't want to take. In the middle of summer it was like five thousand degrees in the desert—there's no way I could survive that *and* two days in the car with my dad and the Stepmonster. All the Stepmonster ever wants to do is rag on me about everything. My hair—magenta with black streaks or black with magenta streaks, depending on your perspective. My tattoos—a Celtic armband, a daisy chain on my ankle, and a heart somewhere the Stepmonster will never see. And what a bad influence I am on Billy, my half brother—who's only a baby for Chrissakes, and who probably thinks my tattoos are cartoons if he even notices them.

On top of it all, it was Labor Day weekend, the last days of freedom before junior year. It was gonna be a big hurrah. I play guitar in this band, Clod, and we were supposed to be in this Indian Summer music festival in Olympia with a bunch of really serious bands, the kind with record contracts. It was the best gig we'd ever gotten and a giant step up from the house parties and cafés we usually played. Of course, Stepmonster wouldn't get that. She thinks punk rock is some kind of devil worship and made me stop practicing in the basement once Billy was born, lest I derange his baby soul. Now I can only practice in Jed's basement, which Stepmonster also doesn't like because Jed is nineteen and lives—*gasp*—with a bunch of people, none of whom are his parents.

So, I politely declined. Okay, maybe not so politely. Maybe my precise words were "I'd rather eat glass," which only caused her to flounce off to Dad, who asked me in that weary way of his why I'd been so rude. I told him about the show. Once upon a time he had cared about things like music, but he just took off his glasses and pinched the bridge of his nose and said it wasn't up for discussion. We were going as a family. I wasn't about to give up that easily. I tried all my tricks: crying, silent treatment, plate throwing. None of it worked. Stepmonster refused to discuss it, so it was just me vs. Dad, and I've never been good at giving him grief, so I had to give in.

I broke the news to my band. Erik, our stoner of a drummer, was just like, "Dude, bummer," but Denise and Jed were really upset. "We've worked so hard—*you've* worked so hard," Jed said, totally breaking my heart with his disappointment. It was true. Three years ago I didn't know a C chord from an F, and now I was booked for a major gig, or should have been. Clod would be playing the Indian Summer Festival as a trio. I was completely crushed I'd be missing it— although it was kind of nice that Jed seemed sad about it.

I should've figured something was fishy when that Friday morning it was just Dad packing up the turd-mobile, the hideous brown minivan Stepmonster insisted they buy when Billy was born. Meanwhile, Stepmonster and Billy were nowhere to be found.

"God, she's always late. You know it's a form of control?"

"Thank you for the psychoanalysis, Brit, but your

mom's not driving with us."

"She's not my mom, and what's the deal? You said it was a family vacation, which is why I *had to go*, had to miss Indian Summer. If they got out of it, I'm not going."

"It is a family vacation," Dad told me, shoving my suitcase into the back. "But two days in a car is too much for Billy. They're going to fly down and meet us."

I really should've known something was *way* fishy when we approached Las Vegas and Dad suggested we stop. Back when Mom was around, this was precisely the kind of thing we'd do. Jump in the car at a moment's notice and drive to Vegas or San Francisco. I remember one night during a heat wave when none of us could sleep; at one in the morning we threw our sleeping bags into the car and drove into the mountains, where there was a perfect breeze. It had been ages since Dad had been cool like that. The Stepmonster had him convinced that spontaneity equaled irresponsibility.

Dad bought me lunch at the fake canals of the Bellagio and even smiled a little when I made fun of some of the fanny-packed tourists. Then we went to a cheesy casino downtown. He said no one would care that I was only sixteen and he gave me twenty bucks to plug into the slot machines. Our little trip was shaping up to be not so bad after all. But when I spied Dad watching me play the slots I couldn't help thinking that he looked, well, empty, like someone had taken a vacuum cleaner and sucked out his soul or something. He didn't even get excited when I won thirty-five bucks, and he insisted on pocketing the money to keep it safe for me. Again, a red flag I didn't notice. Idiot-moron me, for the first time in ages, was just having fun with the Dad I'd been missing for years.

When we left Vegas, he turned quiet and broody, just like he was after everything happened with Mom. I could tell he was squeezing the steering wheel hard, and the whole thing was just so weird and perplexing. I got a little preoccupied with trying to figure out what was up with him, so I didn't notice that we were no longer driving east toward the Grand Canyon, but had turned north into Utah. All I saw out the window was rust-colored clay cliffs, and they seemed Grand Canyon-y enough to me. When we pulled off at some small town just as the sun was going down, I figured we were stopping for the night at another motel, and at first glance Red Rock Academy looked like some crappy value inn: a squat, T-shaped, two-story beige stucco building. Except Red Rock was surrounded by a barbed-wire fence, there was no pool, and the yard was filled with piles of dusty cinder blocks instead of trees. To top it off, there were two freakishly muscular Neanderthals patrolling the grounds.

"What is this?" I asked Dad, smelling the rat strong now.

"It's just a school I want us to take a look at."

"What, like a college? Aren't we jumping the gun a little? I'm only starting junior year."

"No, it's not a college, more like a boarding school."

"For who?"

"For you."

"You want to send me to boarding school?"

"No one's sending you anywhere. We'll just have a look."

"What for? I'm starting school next week, *my* school, back home."

"That's part of it, sweetheart, you haven't been doing so well back at *your* school."

"A couple of C's. Big deal, Dad. It's not the apocalypse."

Dad rubbed his temples. "It's worse than a couple of C's, and it's not just that. Brit, I've been feeling like you aren't a part of our family anymore. You're not *you* anymore, and I want to get you some help before . . ." he trailed off.

"Whoa. You mean you want me to go to this place? Like when?"

"We're just going to take a look," he repeated.

Dad's always been a crappy liar. He blushes and quivers, and I could tell he was full of it. His hands were shaking. The hairs on my arms stood on end. Something was really wrong.

"What in the hell is going on, Dad?" I yelled, and pushed open my car door. My heart was beating fast and hard now, the echo of it pounding in my ears. Then the two muscled freaks were on both sides of me, pinning my arms behind my back and pulling me away from the car.

"Dad! Daddy, what's happening? What are they doing?"

"Please, please be gentle with her," Dad was practically begging the goons. Then he looked at me. "Sweetie, it's for your own good, Brit. Sweetie."

"What are you doing, Dad?" I screamed.

"Where are they taking me?"

"It's for your own good, Brit," he said again, and I could tell he was crying, which scared me even more.

I was shoved into a small, stuffy room, and the door was locked behind me. Hiccupping sobs, I waited for my dad to realize he'd made a terrible mistake and come get me. But he didn't. I heard him talking to some woman. I heard our car start and then the sound of the motor faded. I started bellowing all over again, my face streaming with tears and snot and spit. I cried, but no one came for me. I cried until I could do nothing else but fall asleep. When I woke up, maybe an hour later, I'd forgotten where I was. I remembered with a start and with a clear understanding of why I was locked up. Stepmonster. She did this to me. My fear and sadness were nothing compared with my fury at her. And then there was something else. A sinking feeling of disappointment. In spite of it all, I'd actually been looking forward to seeing the Grand Canyon.

Chapter 2

"Oppositional defiance disorder." Red Rock had assigned me a shrink, and ODD is what she insisted I had. We were sitting in her dark office decorated with weird posters that I guess were supposed to be inspirational. One had a bunch of geese flying in formation and a caption that read, "With a plan in place, you can go miles." Funny. I couldn't go miles because they'd taken away my clothes and my shoes so I wouldn't run away. I was wearing pajamas and slippers in the middle of the afternoon.

My shrink droned on, reading from a big, fat book that apparently contained all the secrets of the mind. "'Often loses temper, often argues with adults, actively defies or refuses to comply with adults' requests or rules, deliberately annoys people, blames others for his or her mistakes or misbehavior, is often angry and resentful, is often spiteful and vindictive . . .'"

"Does that sound familiar?" she asked. She looked like a pilgrim. She was skinny and had a bowl haircut and was dressed in this high-necked ruffled blouse even though it was broiling in her office.

I was pretty out of it, as you can imagine. I'd been up all night, stuck in my little room until the goons came to deliver me to some equally burly nurse. I'd immediately christened her Helga. Helga confiscated my iPod and all of my jewelry, even my belly-button ring, ignoring my protests that the hole would close up, forcing me to get it re-pierced. After she'd put my jewelry in an envelope, she ordered me to strip and stayed there while I did. She put on gloves and started feeling me up under my armpits and in my mouth. Then she made me bend over while she looked *down there*—front and back. I'd never even had a gyno exam so this freaked me out beyond words and I started to cry. Helga didn't even give me a tissue. She just kept on pawing around down there, looking for drugs I figured, even though that's so not my scene. Pot makes me tired and alcohol makes me puke. No thanks.

Anyhow, by the time the shrink woman—Dr. Clayton—had started telling me about my disorder that morning, I was too out of it to point out that her ODD description summed up just about every teenager I knew. All I could say was, "I take it you heard all this from my Stepmonster," at which she smiled and wrote more stuff down on her clipboard.

"Let me put it to you in terms you understand. Your grades at school have dropped. You are hardly present. You stay out all night. And when you do show your face, you're as pleasant as a dark cloud."

"I am not. And when I stay out late it's because of *shows*. When you're low on the totem pole, you get the two-A.M. slot. By the time we pack up our gear and get home it's five A.M., but it's not like I'm out partying all night."

Dr. Clayton didn't say anything, just shot me a Stepmonster-like disapproving look and wrote some more stuff down before continuing her list of my so-called offenses.

"You treat your body like a wall to graffiti on. You

are rude to your stepmother, sullen to your teachers, unkind to your brother, and you seem to have some unresolved feelings about your mother."

"Don't you dare talk about my mother," I said, surprised by how much like a growl my voice sounded. At the mere mention of Mom, I felt a chill grip me, and tears sprang to my eyes. I immediately blinked them back. "You don't get to talk about her."

"I see," Dr. Clayton said, adding to her scribbles. "Well then, shall we go over the ground rules?" she asked, all sing-songy, like she was explaining a fun game. "We work on a rewards and levels system here. As a new student, you will start out in Level One. Level One is mostly an evaluatory stage, so the staff can get a sense of who you are and what your difficulties are. It's also a chance for you to start proving yourself. There are very few privileges in Level One. You will remain indoors in an isolated room. You will do schoolwork in your room and have your meals there. You will leave only for individual therapy and to use the bathroom. To ensure you do no harm to yourself, you will be supervised at all times.

"You will graduate to Level Two when we have

ascertained that you are not a runaway risk and that you are ready to start working on your issues. At Level Two, you will get your shoes back. You will leave your room for meals and for group therapy sessions. You may also receive mail from family at the staff's discretion.

"Things improve once you arrive at Level Three. You will be moved into a shared room, allowed to attend school in a classroom, and permitted to send and receive mail, corresponding with family members only. You will also participate in many more activities. In Level Four you may wear makeup and receive phone calls from persons preapproved by our staff. When you reach Level Five you may have family visits and participate in organized town outings, like movie nights and bowling.

"Level Six is the highest level. Earning Level Six status would enable you to lead therapy groups, even supervise new students, and go off campus. Once you complete Level Six, you'll return home, but that's a long way off. It can take months to reach Level Six, or years. That part's up to you. Any time you misbehave, break rules, or refuse to fully participate in your therapy, you will be demoted a level or two. If the situation warrants it, you could even get yourself demoted to Level One."

She smiled when she said the last bit, and you could tell she got off on the thought of it.

Chapter 3

After four days in isolation, I started sprouting under-arm hair. Red Rock Academy policy did not allow anyone under Level Five to use a razor. The logic behind this is unclear. I have never heard of a girl doing harm to herself or others with a Ladyshaver. But when I went into the empty bathroom to take my first shower—supervised by a staff member who watched me the whole time—I was given a bottle of baby shampoo and that was it. No combs. No razors. Level Three permitted electric razors—I guess they weren't worried about us electrocuting ourselves to death—but until then, I had to go native.

Among the other indignities of Level One was the

constant supervision, even when I used the toilet. At night the guards watched me, but during the day it was a steady stream of Level Sixers. Some of them were bitchy and condescending, lording their mighty status over me. I hated them. Others were nice and condescending, full of pep talks about keeping with the program. I hated them even more.

So I spent my early days at Red Rock empathizing with how zoo animals must feel. The only thing I had to do was read the lame-ass school primers they gave me, filled with stuff like geometry. I did geometry in ninth grade! I was literally bored to tears, but there was no way I was going to let anyone see me cry.

Instead of Dr. Clayton, I'd been having sessions with the director of the place, a kind of tough-love guru named Bud Austin. "But you can call me Sheriff. Everyone does," he told me. "I used to be a cop, but now I take care of the real hardened cases: you girls." He laughed. It was my first day of solitary and he'd come for a visit, dragging in a metal folding chair. He was tall with black hair and a bushy mustache. He wore too-tight jeans with a ton of keys hanging from one belt loop, and lizard cowboy boots poked out beneath the cuffed bottoms.

"Now let me tell you a secret," he continued with his pat, one-size-fits-all speech. "You're probably gonna hate me at first. All the girls do. But let me tell you, one day you're gonna grow up some and realize that Red Rock is the best thing that ever happened to you, and I'm one of the most important people you'll meet here. Hell, you might even invite me to your wedding." All I could think was, *Wedding?* I'm only sixteen! But he just went on. "Your parents have gone soft, is my guess. That's why so many girls get out of control—that, and for attention. You're gonna get plenty of that here. Because, girlie," (that's what he called you, either that or your last name, never by your first name) "we're gonna refocus your misdirected life. We're gonna challenge your attitude, and we're gonna replace your inappropriate behaviors with productive ones. In other words, we're gonna straighten you out. It might not seem like it, but we love you."

The next day Sheriff came into my little room again, dragging his little chair. "Girlie, you ready to face yourself?" This struck me as the dumbest question in the world. Face what exactly? It was as if he'd already decided I was a delusional moron. So I just said, "I'd need a mirror for that. But I guess breakable reflective glass would be too dangerous for a psycho like me." Sheriff stood up, folded his chair and left the room, clicking the bolt on the door behind him. The next afternoon, it was the same spiel: "Hemphill, ready to face yourself?" "Oh, go to hell," I said. The third day, when he showed up with his chair and his question, I wanted to tell him to face my middle finger, but something kept me from saying anything at all. So he gave me a little lecture about doing things the hard way or the easy way. I seriously wanted to laugh because he was *so* full of it, except that I also wanted to cry because this idiot was in charge of me.

I kept up as brave a face as I could, refusing to give any of them—Sheriff, Helga, Stepmonster, the bitchy Sixers—the satisfaction of seeing me down. But at night, when the last light went out and my door was locked from the outside, I cried until my pillow was soaked through.

Finally, after the Sheriff's fifth visit, when my armpit hairs were nearly braidable, one of the Level Sixers opened my door. She was tall, with a striking angular face framed by dirty blond hair. It was cut in a funky choppy style that seemed too high maintenance for our prison. Maybe Sixers got salon privileges.

"Look, Brit. That is your name, right?" she asked me with the kind of exasperated impatience teachers reserve for their slowest pupils. "Well, Brit, maybe you enjoy wearing your pj's in solitary confinement, but if you don't, cut the Rebel-Without-a-Cause crap. No one here is impressed by it."

"I don't know what you're talking about."

"Spare me. Just tell Sheriff you're ready to face yourself. That's all it takes to get to Level Two."

"Seriously?"

She arched an eyebrow at me, letting me know what a dunce she thought I was. "I've got better things to do than sit here guarding your door. Just say you're ready to face yourself. It doesn't matter if it's true. Do us all a favor and check your pride at your cell door."

This turned out to be one of the most valuable lessons I would learn at Red Rock.

Chapter 4

"You're a drunk."

"You're a slut."

"Whore. Whore. Whore."

It was my third week at Red Rock, and along with about twenty other girls, I was in one of two therapy centers: giant empty rooms with dirty windows, blue gymnastics pads on the floor, and more fading inspirational posters. (My personal fave: a cat hanging on to a tree. "He can because he thinks he can." Um, no, he can because he's got claws.) There was no furniture. Guess they didn't want us to go all Jerry Springer and start hurling it around.

Like the rest of the inmates, I was wearing the

required uniform: khaki shorts and a Red Rock polo shirt—an outfit that I'm convinced was designed as a form of fashion punishment. We were all standing in a circle, looking like a suburban high-school phys-ed class. At the center of the circle a girl named Sharon was giving us a deer-in-the-headlights look as she turned to catch insult after insult. A counselor named Deirdre and a Level Sixer named Lisa egged us on. "Tell her what you think. Ask her why she sleeps around. Ask her why she doesn't respect herself."

Welcome to "confrontational therapy." It's supposed to make you face your issues, but it mostly makes you cry—which seems to be the point because it was only after you'd cried that you were allowed to leave the circle and "process" what just happened. CT, as it's called, was a big crowd-pleaser at Red Rock, very gladiator-like, and those who'd been inside the circle were even more vicious once they found themselves safely outside it. For example, the girl chanting "whore" was Shana, who only a week ago had been berated for her eating disorder—until she broke down sobbing and was promptly rewarded with a group hug.

I'd pretty quickly figured out that CT was typical

of the Red Rock philosophy: Treat ODD teenagers like crap until they break. Now that I was in Level Two, my days were spent in CT, in strange lecturey one-on-ones with Sheriff or another one of the counselors, and—once a week—with Dr. Clayton, who'd already suggested putting me on antidepressants. I *was* depressed now, but only because I was at Red Rock. The rest of my days were spent back in my cell, doing "self-directed" study, which was the academic equivalent of Mad Libs, even though back at school I would've been in AP English. I still wasn't able to write to my dad or get any letters from him. That wouldn't happen until Level Three, when I'd be sprung from my room and allowed to attend school.

●　●　●

"Brit, right?"

Beside me in the confrontation circle stood the Sixer who'd taught me the key to escaping Level One. She was scarily tall, towering over me, and giving me that same you're-an-idiot face she had before. I was really starting to hate the Level Sixers, who generally seemed like a bunch of do-goodery, kiss-ass snobs.

"I believe we've established that's my name," I told her.

She arched her eyebrows again. "Well, Brit. Mouth it."

"Huh?"

"Mouth it. Pretend you're saying something."

"What?"

"Do you not understand English or are you just slow? You're not 'participating in the process.'" She was whispering, but she made it sound like a barked order.

"I don't know anything about this girl. I can't yell at her."

"Are you moronic or deaf? Mouth it. Fake it. Or you'll get in trouble. Have I made myself clear?"

Before I had a chance to think of a clever reply, she had moved to the other side of the circle, where she was chanting insults so ferociously that you had to watch closely to see that she wasn't actually making a sound.

I didn't know what to make of her. She was a total bitch to me, insulting me as much as the counselors did, telling me how delusional I was. She might have been trying to railroad me: You could move up levels

23

at Red Rock by narcing out your roommates (so Fascist). But her advice *was* kind of subversive, which had me thinking she was maybe trying to help. I did what she told me to, and it turned out to be her second piece of good advice. After I started fake name-calling in group, one of the counselors patted me on the back and said I'd begun to "work my program." When I met with Dr. Clayton later that week, she gave me a creepy smile and said she thought I was finally ready to "deal with my demons" and "break down my walls." Which meant promotion to Level Three, and *real* school—a windowless room with a dozen desks where I'd do more self-directed study while watched by guards who didn't look like they could spell their own names. I was also moved into a shared room with three other inmates: a fat girl named Martha, a rich, snooty waif named Bebe, and blonde, bulimic Tiffany, who alternated between hysterical smiliness and hysterical tears.

When I wasn't in school, therapy, or meals, I was doing physical therapy. This consisted of spending four hours in the hot desert heat dragging five-pound cinder blocks from a giant pile across fifty feet of dusty yard and stacking them into a wall. Sounds like pure torture, I know, but it actually wasn't so bad. I mean, for sure my muscles killed me at first, and we worked without gloves, so my hands turned bloody and then all callused. Plus, the work made me thirsty and I had to drink a ton of water but could only pee once an hour. Still, the counselors-cum-guards were lazy and preferred to stay in the shade, so the cinder-block yard was the one place that us inmates could talk freely amongst ourselves.

"This is ruining my hands," Bebe bitched. "My nails used to be so pretty."

"Can it, Rodeo Drive," scolded the Level Four girl next to her.

"How many times do I have to spell this out for you, yokel. Rodeo Drive is in Beverly Hills, and it's where podunk tourists shop. I don't even live in Beverly Hills. I live in the Palisades. So shut it already." Everyone called Bebe "Rodeo Drive." People were jealous of her, I gathered, because she was so pretty with her long, shiny black hair and blue catlike eyes. Her mom was Marguerite Howarth, a famous soap-opera actress. Bebe had been my room-mate for two days but hadn't deigned to speak to me, so I wasn't about to put myself in her line of fire. But it was obviously my lucky day.

"Where are you from?" she asked me.

"Oregon. Portland."

"I've been there. Rain and people wearing the most unattractive flannel."

I happened to love Portland and didn't appreciate LA people dissing it, but I had to admit she was right about the flannel.

"And what are you in for?"

"No idea."

"Oh, come now. You must have some idea, my dear girl. Bulimia? Promiscuous behavior? Self-mutilation?" Bebe said, ticking off potential abuses.

"None of the above."

"Well, let's see. You have the hair and the tattoos. If I were to take a wild stab in the dark, I'd say you're a musician or an artist."

"Musician," was all I said, but inwardly I was kind of surprised. My mom had been the artist.

"Ahh, heroin? Meth?" Bebe ventured.

"No, none of those. I just play in a band, have pink hair, and have a freak of a stepmother."

"Ahh, we have a Cinderella in the house!" Bebe called to the crowd before turning her attention back to me. "How very Disney. What did Clayton diagnose you as during your intake?"

"Opposition something something."

"Oppositional defiance disorder. You're ODD," said a sure voice from behind. It was the girl again, the tall bitchy Sixer with the good advice. "We *all* get tagged with that label. It's a no-brainer. What're your other offenses?"

"I don't know."

She sighed. "Okay, newbie. Let me give you the remedial catch-up. Red Rock inmates fall into five broad categories: You've got your substance abusers, but never anything worse than pot or ecstasy because a weekly AA meeting is all the drug treatment this place offers. Then there are your sexual deviants, comprising slutty girls and dykes. Cassie over there"—she pointed to a girl with short red hair and freckles—"is in on lesbo watch, and Bebe here is in on slut watch—she got caught making it with the pool boy."

"That's not entirely accurate, my darling Virginia," Bebe said, shaking her long mane of hair. "I got caught making it with the *Mexican* pool boy. That was my real offense. An unthinkable crossing of class lines."

"Thanks for the clarification, Karl Marx. And don't call me Virginia. I go by V."

"V is not a name, darling; it's a letter."

"And BB is two letters. What's your point? Now where was I? Yes. The food issues. Mostly minor-league bulimics. Red Rock would never take on any serious anorexics because they need serious help, not the fraudulent counseling that passes for therapy here. Do you know, Clayton's the only one around here with any credentials? And she's not even a shrink. She's an internist. She's only here to prescribe pills. So we just get a smattering of occasional throw-up dieters and a lot of obese girls whose parents think that Red Rock is more "therapeutic" than fat camp.

"Our precious roomie, Martha, for instance," Bebe said. "She's a fat-camper."

"Correct," said V. "Then we have a handful of cutters—you know, the self-mutilating types. And a grab bag of your garden-variety runaways and petty thieves—we've got lots of kleptos here. And last but not least, the suicidal-ideation girls."

"Like our Virginia," Bebe said.

"You? You tried to kill yourself?" I asked.

"No. Too Sylvia Plath. If I had, Red Rock would've been afraid to let me in. I just wrote some poems and stories about a girl who kills herself. Spooked my mom enough to send me away. And I've been here ever since. Almost a year and a half."

"V is for *veteran*." Bebe smirked.

"No, V is for *Virginia*, and for *victory* and for *vixen*."

"You're incorrigible, you bad, bad girl. I'm so impressed," Bebe faked a yawn.

"Sarcasm creates a chasm between yourself and others," V said with mock piousness. She turned to me. "Another Red Rock nugget of wisdom. Anyway, I'm in Level Six now and I intend to be back home before Christmas."

"Where's home?"

"Manhattan."

"Back to work, ladies. Cut the chitchat," one of the counselors yelled from the patio, where she was reading a copy of *Us Weekly*.

"Ugh," Bebe groaned. "They really need to provide us with sunblock. When I have to Botox, I'm going to bill Red Rock for each and every wrinkle."

"Hey, look, we finished the wall," I said. We'd

been so busy talking, I hadn't noticed that every last cinder block was stacked up neatly. Bebe and V looked at each other, laughing at me.

"Yes, the wall is finished. And now we break it down," V said.

"The wall is meant to teach us that our existence is futile, dears," Bebe said. "Welcome to Red Rock logic."

Later that night in our dorm, I asked Bebe which soap her mom had been on. She narrowed her eyes at me and turned away, like I'd asked some ridiculously inappropriate personal question. I didn't get her. Or V, either. They were like Jekyll and Hyde, giving advice one minute and icing me the next. I was starting to think it might be better to keep to myself, because after Bebe snubbed me, I'd felt worse than I had when I took my first fully supervised shower. I even cried into my pillow that night, something I hadn't done in weeks. The next morning, though, I found a note tucked into the pocket of my Red Rock shirt.

Cinderella, the walls have eyes (notice the cameras?) and ears (beware of Tiffany). Ratting is a way of life

around here. No chat in the building.
Cinder-block yard only.
   BB

I crumpled up the note and smiled. Someone had my back.

Chapter 5

When I was growing up, I never had the sense that someone had my back, because I never knew what it was like when someone didn't. It would never have occurred to me that I could end up alone and vulnerable, since in those days, my family was the best, the coolest, the tightest.

My parents met at a U2 concert. Dad was working as a roadie, and Bono pulled my mom onstage to dance. He used to do that at every concert. Every girl in the audience probably thought she was worthy, but Mom *really* was. She had this thing about her, this light—an energy that made you want to be around her because when you were, life was giddy. *Free spirit* is such a clichéd term, but it totally fit my mom. When she went floating backstage that night, she looked up at Dad in her post-Bono ecstasy and kissed him. He was probably a goner right there and then.

After that, it was like some bohemian fairy tale. They tromped around Europe and Africa together, with Mom selling her paintings to earn money. They got married on a cliff top in Morocco, and she got pregnant with me in a Portobello Road hotel in London—hence my name, Brit (middle name is Paula for Bono, whose real name is Paul). Then they moved to Portland and bought a ramshackle house on Salmon Street and started CoffeeNation, a coffee-house/art gallery/club.

I don't know how many kids can say that they once crayoned in a Muppets coloring book with Kurt Cobain, but I can. Tons of musicians and artists hung around CoffeeNation, which was funny because neither Mom nor Dad knew an A from an A minor. But they had a weekly open-mic night, and a lot of bands got their start there, and I think the place just got a reputation as a music haven.

We pretty much lived at CoffeeNation. After school, I'd sit down at my own reserved table, and

Dad would fix me a hot chocolate before I started my homework. It never took me long because I had like forty pseudo big brothers and sisters there to help me—musicians are weirdly good at math, which is probably one reason that back in my own school, I would've been taking calculus in my junior year. My favorite customer was Reggie, a tattoo artist whose arms, legs, and torso were like a mosaic. A lot of people probably thought he looked like a thug, but he was the nicest guy ever. He loved to read almost as much as he liked to talk, and he used to check out a copy of whatever book I was reading for school, so we could have literary discussions together. I was only eight when we met, and Reggie and I read *Are You There God? It's Me, Margaret.* together.

When my friends complained about their parents, I didn't even pretend to agree. I hung out with my parents most afternoons at the café until Mom and I went home to cook up these wild dinners—like the night she decided everything had to be purple (eggplant stew with beets and grapes isn't half bad, by the way). We'd eat late when Dad got home, and I never got sick of being around them.

Just before seventh-grade winter break, Mom got

it in her head that we should escape the gray and go live on the beach in Mexico for a month. She whispered her idea into Dad's ear, and next thing you know, Grandma is running CoffeeNation, and we're living in huts on the Yucatan Peninsula, eating fish tacos for breakfast. What kind of parents let their kids do something like that, even if it means missing a couple weeks of school?

Looking back, to tell the truth, I guess Mom didn't care quite enough about stuff like school, but Dad did. Where she was like a rainbow after a storm, he was like the umbrella during it—the solid one keeping us dry: the doctor-appointment maker, the lunch packer, the worrier. Dad was the parent, and Mom was more like another kid. So maybe that's why when she started to change, no one noticed at first. She'd do odd things, like insist that we unplug all the phones and leave on the downstairs lights at night—to prevent spies from watching us, she'd say. Or she'd leave for work and show up at CoffeeNation four hours later, with no memory of where she'd been. When she took a knife to her paintings because "the voices told me to," we started with all the doctors and their diagnoses. First "borderline personality disorder." Then "paranoia." And finally "paranoid schizophrenia." But Mom refused to admit anything was wrong and refused any treatment. My grandma moved up from California to take care of us and begged Dad to have Mom committed to a mental hospital, but Dad just kept saying, "Not yet; she might get better." I think he really believed that. Until the day she left us.

After that, Dad had to close down CoffeeNation and go to work at a software company, which is where he met Stepmonster, who's the kind of woman who freaks out if her handbag doesn't match her shoes perfectly. Within a year they were married, and my wonderful family was history. Then I understood that having someone watch your back isn't automatic. It's special—and it can be taken away from you.

Chapter 6

"How'd they get you?" Bebe asked. It was my second week working the cinder-block piles. Autumn had arrived suddenly, cooling the desert furnace and making the sky turn an unbelievable shade of blue.

"How did *who* get me?"

Out of the corner of my eye I saw V snicker. She and Bebe had some kind of weird friendship—constantly insulting each other affectionately—and because Bebe and I were roommates, I ended up spending a lot of time around V. Unfortunately, everything I did seemed to irritate her.

"Cassie, this is our ignorant newbie, Brit. Have you met?"

"We've howdied but that's all. Nice to meet ya."

"You too." Cassie was from Texas, strong like a ranch hand, and great to work near on the quarry.

"Red Rock, darling," Bebe explained. "How'd you get here?" she asked again.

"My dad drove me. How else would I get here?"

"An escort, of course," Bebe said.

"Like a date?" I asked. V laughed again, right in my face this time.

"Now don't laugh, V," Cassie said, giving me a sympathetic look. "More like a kidnappin'. That's how they got me. They came for me in the middle of the night and hauled me away like a stray dog or somethin'. They even handcuffed me. I thought it was some kind of abduction, until I caught sight of my folks watchin' from the window."

"They did it because you're . . . gay."

"Well, they think I am."

"Are you?"

"I'm bi. But don't get all squirrelly on me. You don't hit on every guy you meet, so it's not like I'm gonna come after you." She was right about that. I didn't hit on *any* guy I met. I just crushed hopelessly after Jed.

"It's nice to see that Cassie's given you her introductory homophobia lecture. Forgive her," V said. "She can't help herself."

"Yeah, well, half the girls in this place act like they think I'm checking them out all the time. And most of them ain't even cute."

"But you were kidnapped and brought here? That's awful, Cassie."

"Darling Brit," Bebe interrupted. "It's called an escort, and it's standard operating procedure."

"So your parents did that too?"

"Parent, singular. Dad's out of the picture. And Mother, well there's no Four Seasons within a hundred miles of this place. She wouldn't be caught dead here."

"Are your parents rich, Brit?" V asked.

"That's none of your business." I could tell that V's were. She had that money smell to her.

"Don't get all *OC* on me, newbie. I ask because if you have money, you're screwed. Insurance pays for the first three months of your stay. If you're poor, then suddenly at three months, boom, you're in level Six and out the door. Cured by the miracle of Scam Rocks. But if your family has the money to keep

footing the bill, that's an entirely different set of cir-
cumstances. You could be stuck for life."

"Don't be so dramatic, Virginia. Until you're
eighteen," Bebe said. She looked at my panicked face.
"When you're eighteen, you can check yourself out."

"How long have you all been here?"

"Six months," Cassie said. "My parents aren't
rich, but they're desperate to straighten me out."

"Four months," Bebe said. "But you can guarantee I'll be here or at some other school a while. I've
been at boarding schools for years. Of course, this is
my first RTC."

"RTC?"

"God, newbie," said V. "It's a residential treatment center. They call it a school, but it's a loony bin,
a bogus, bullshit, behavior-modification boot-camp
warehouse for unwanted misfit teens."

Argh! Sometimes I really wanted to hurl a brick at
V, to knock that all-knowing expression right off her
face. My dad would never shuttle me off to boot
camp. The thought of it made me want to cry. "My
dad doesn't want me warehoused!" I said defiantly.

"Right," V said. "He just sent you here to rest up.
Sure he did."

"It wasn't the dad," Bebe pointed out. "She's a Cinderella story. The stepmom sent her here."

"I'd reckon your stepmom reads *LifeStyle* magazine," Cassie said.

She did. There were stacks of them in our kitchen. She claimed she liked the recipes.

"Red Rock advertises in the back, promising quick results to cure the surly child," Bebe said. "You can't totally blame your stepmom, though. They make this place seem like a therapeutic Club Med."

"That's why they encourage the escorts instead of drop-offs. They don't much appreciate parents seein' this place in its skivvies," Cassie added with a sly smile.

"That's also why they monitor your mail. To preempt any complaints you may have," V said. "There's this whole section in the brochure warning parents to expect their kids to complain about how badly they're treated here. Our lies are part of our sickness. It's pretty clever. They really know how to cover their asses."

"Oh my God, it's a total gulag."

"That is the first smart thing you've said, Brit." V tapped me on the forehead. "Of course, every gulag has its secrets, escape routes, and codes."

"What do you mean?"

"There are ways to subvert the power."

"*What?*"

"Patience, newbie. You'll learn," V said.

"All will be revealed," Bebe promised.

Cassie put her hands together and bowed forward like a Tibetan monk who knew the secrets of the universe, and we all cracked up. It was the first time I'd laughed at Red Rock. But then the guards heard us having too much fun and separated us.

Chapter 7

Out in the yard, you'd think no one was paying attention, but Bebe was right—there were eyes everywhere. The next time I had my appointment with Clayton, she immediately brought up V.

"I hear you are spending a lot of time with Virginia Larson," she said. "You girls call her V, I'm told."

"We sometimes build cinder-block walls together, and sometimes we take down those walls. If that's how you define spending time."

"Brit, you may think your quips are winning but they are only self-defeating. In any case, I would discourage you from getting close to Virginia."

"But why? She's Level Six. Isn't she supposed to be

a positive influence on me?" I still wasn't sure whether V was friend or foe, but Clayton's warning made me lean toward the former.

"Virginia is Level Six for now. But she has a way of backsliding, so, no, I don't think I'd qualify her as a positive influence. Now, I need your word that you'll steer clear of her, and if you give it to me, it will prove that you are responsible enough."

"Responsible enough for what?"

"To get a letter from your father. I've had it a while but I didn't think you were ready."

What right did she have to withhold mail from my dad? I wanted to lunge across the desk and wring her skinny neck until her pilgrim head popped off. But I wanted the letter even more. I bit my lip. I was doing a lot of that lately, so much so that part of it was turning purple. I told her I'd avoid Virginia, so she handed me the letter, watching me expectantly. As if I would open it in front of her. No way. I held on to it until dinner.

Dear Brit:

I hope this letter finds you well. Fall has arrived in Portland, and we've had rain every day. No sooner does it get light than it gets dark. Never my favorite time of year. The drainpipes have already clogged with leaves and flooded the living room again. Your mother has been busy taking care of the repairs.

We are all fine. Billy misses you. He crawls to your room and likes to sit outside your door. It's sweet.

Your friends from the band were very upset by your absence. Jed and Denise have come over several times to look for you, and when I finally explained where you were, Denise grew quite angry. I suppose I understand. No one likes the ogre who breaks up the group. Jed asked if he could write to you, but I told him you were not allowed to receive mail from non–family members. He insisted that I give you a message about a song you wrote. In fact, he refused to leave until I swore on your health that I'd tell you that they would not forget the Firefly song. I don't quite understand the big deal as

you're not in the band anymore, but a
promise is a promise.

I expect you are very angry with me
and your mother, but I hope in my heart of
hearts that one day you might understand
that this was done from love.

I know you can't write me yet, but
when you are allowed to, I hope you will.

Happy Halloween.

I love you,

Dad

Up until that point, I'd been left out of the CT circles, but two days after I got my letter from Dad, Sheriff decided to lead group. And guess whose turn it was for the hot seat? Sheriff played it like a twisted game of duck, duck, goose, standing at the head of the confrontation circle, cocking an imaginary trigger with his finger, squinting like he was looking through a rifle sight. "Which one of you little girls thinks you can hide from the truth?" he asked in his gruff cowboy voice. "You? You? You?" he asked while he pointed at each of us. Then he stopped on me and motioned me to the middle.

"Why, Miss Hemphill, I don't think we've heard from you. Word has it you got a letter from your papa. You got anything to say about that?"

I knew what I was supposed to say: that the letter made me angry, that I hated my father for dumping me here. It was standard CT hazing practice to start in with the obvious. The thing was, the letter *had* made me angry. Angry that Dad was making Red Rock seem like his decision, angry that he insisted on calling Step-monster "your mother" as though saying it would make it true and erase what came before. And angry that he assumed that Clod was broken up, and I was out of it—as if that had been his grand scheme. But then, a tiny part of me felt bad for being mad. Because while I was furious with the After Dad, the one who'd let Stepmonster shove me off to this place, I could never fully forget my once-upon-a-time Before Dad. Before Dad was the gentle worrywart I'd grown up with, the heartbroken softy who'd fallen to bits when Mom went crazy. Before Dad was a pushover, only back then it was Mom he adored like a kid loves his new puppy. After Dad was a pushover for Stepmonster.

"It seems Miss Hemphill needs a little encouragement from you girlies," Sheriff said. "Maybe one of you can get inside that angry little head of hers. My goodness, could she be so angry that she's turning red right to the tips of her hair?"

I heard the girls in the circle titter. As if magenta streaks were the freakiest thing they could imagine. Whatever. Pink streaks are not a form of rebellion. Lots of my parents' CoffeeNation friends had neon hair, and Mom used to help me dye my hair with food coloring when I was a kid.

Besides, I didn't even care about what anyone said—even Sheriff, who tended to scare me as much as he infuriated me. I was too busy thinking about Dad's letter—the little gift he'd inadvertently put in it. Because though "Firefly" is a song, I'm not the one who wrote it.

• • •

It's always seemed like some sort of miracle that I got to be in Clod. Jed, Denise, and Erik were not only years older than me, they were all competent musicians—Jed on guitar, Denise on bass, and Erik on drums. I, on the other hand, was fifteen when I first tried out for the band, and to say I sucked at guitar at that point was a compliment.

Learning to play had been one of my Stepmonster-avoidance strategies. When she and Dad got married, she quit her job, so she was home all the time, redecorating the kitchen, talking on the phone to her sister in Chicago, making me feel like I no longer belonged there. So I did my best not to be there. I lingered after school. Spent hours nursing coffees at a greasy-spoon restaurant. Then one weekend I picked up a second-hand electric guitar and amplifier at a yard sale. I holed up in the basement, learning to play from a book, trying not to remember the days when I would've had twenty musicians lining up to teach me.

I'd been playing all of five months when I saw the notice at the X-Ray Cafe: PUNK-POP POWER TRIO SEEKS RHYTHM GUITAR PLAYER. Considering my lack of experience, I was pretty nervous when I arrived at Jed's house to try out, and when I first laid eyes on him, my nerves turned to full-on jitters. Jed was tall and lanky with adorably sloppy brown hair that curled over the nape of his neck. His eyes were green, with a glint of warm brown in the middle. I'd been around cute rock guys all the time at CoffeeNation, but something about Jed totally flustered me. I turned away from him and busied myself plugging my guitar into my amp, but I was so distracted that I didn't notice the amp was turned way up. Then I heard the feedback loop bouncing against the walls.

"Yow!" screamed Denise. She had bleached blond hair and eyes that dared you to mess with her.

"Cool," Erik shouted. "I think she dislodged some earwax."

The feedback was still blaring. "Do you want to turn that down?" Jed shouted. I continued to stand there like a moron. Jed had to click off the amp himself. "I think we've established that you can make some good feedback," he said.

"Yep," I said, snapping out of my haze. "I was practically raised on the Velvet Underground, so it's in my blood."

Jed smiled at that. "Okay. Let's hear how you play. We're going to do 'Badlands.' It's pretty basic. GCD. Listen and fall in when you're ready."

At first I was hesitant to jump in, and when I finally did I sort of tripped over myself for a few chords. But then the weirdest thing happened. I relaxed, and something clicked. I may have been the worst guitar player in

Portland at that point, but with Clod, I rocked.

Jed called me a few days later to tell me I was in. "Boy, you must have had some crappy candidates," I joked.

Jed chuckled. Even through the phone his laugh was warm and rumbly. "No. We had some very talented musicians. But four people playing instruments perfectly doesn't necessarily translate into a good band," he said. "I dunno. We all liked your vibe. And you were definitely the best at distortion."

"Thanks. I've been working on that," I said, and Jed laughed again. "While we're sharing, I should probably tell you that I can't play bar chords."

I heard him sigh, but he didn't waver. "We'll want to work on that," he said. "Bar chords can be important."

As soon as I started playing with Clod, it was like I'd always been in the band—even with my deficiencies, which Jed helped me to overcome. After practice, Denise and Erik would go upstairs for a bagel or a beer while Jed stayed behind, going over whatever parts of the songs I was having trouble with. Sometimes he'd lean over me to position my hand on the fretboard, and I could feel the hair on his arm tickling mine. It was pretty much impossible to keep my mind on the music.

I practiced every day until my fingertips turned first raw and then hard like leather. I got better, a lot better, fast. When I mastered bar chords, Jed did this little absentminded nod and smile. And then he insisted I start working on vocals.

"I can't sing," I told him.

"Yes you can."

"No, really. I can't."

"Brit, I should let you in on a secret," Jed said. "You are *always* singing. Songs. TV jingles, you name it. And when you've got your headphones on, you sing *really* loud."

"No joke," Erik said, laughing.

"We've all heard you," Denise added. "You've got voice."

So, I started singing a couple of the songs. Then I started writing lyrics. Then I started writing riffs to go along with my lyrics. And then suddenly Clod was playing *my* songs. And I couldn't help but notice that more often than not, Jed did that little nod-smile thing at me.

• • •

"Brit, you're in denial. And I'm not talking about a river in Egypt."

I jerked my head up. A Level Four girl named Kimberly was glaring at me. Sheriff loved that stupid denial joke. That little suckup probably just bought her ticket to Level Five at my expense.

"That's right. You know you're gonna have to come clean sometime," Sheriff said. "Might as well stop wasting all our time. 'Cause that moment of reckoning is coming soon. Ain't that right, girls?"

"It is."

"Coming soon."

"Happens to us all."

"Gotta look into the mirror."

The chorus of psychobabble went on. I tuned it out and went back into my head.

• • •

I knew it was pointless to be in love with Jed. At the end of every show, there was always a handful of girls waiting by the backstage door: cool-looking girls with sleek black bangs, funky granny glasses, or buzz cuts and nose rings. After we loaded our stuff, sometimes Jed would slip away to meet with one of them. Occasionally, I'd think he had a girlfriend, but the gig-girls never seemed to last longer than a few weeks. *See,* I told myself. *It's better to be his friend, his protégé, his little sister than some two-week stand.* That was how I comforted myself, anyhow.

I was so grateful to have the band in my life. Especially once Stepmonster saw the double blue line on her pregnancy test. Then and there, whatever respect she'd had for Dad's and my relationship vanished, and suddenly it was like I became the competition. She started talking to Dad about me right in front of me, about my bad grades, my late hours, my being too young to be in a band.

She should've been glad about Clod. It was the only thing that kept me from heaving her off the Hawthorne Bridge. I was a mess at practices back then. I'd start crying mid-set or just flub a song I knew really well. I was sure they'd chuck me from the band, but instead they'd stop playing, Jed would make a pot of coffee, and they'd wait for me to calm down. Denise would ad-lib funny songs about Stepmonster on her bass to try to cheer me up. Erik would offer me a bong load.

I lived for those practices and our shows, when we'd all pile into Jed's Vanagon, stopping at a taqueria near his house for pre-show burritos. Then we'd play, usually a house party or a coffeehouse, but sometimes even a twenty-one-and-over club. Being up on stage, watching people totally rocking out to what we were doing, I felt that same sense of clicking that I'd experienced when I tried out for Clod, only a thousand times stronger. After the shows, we'd all be hyper and we'd pack up our stuff and go to Denny's to pig out on pancakes and coffee. I'd go home feeling happy, like I belonged, like I still had a family.

The day Stepmonster went into labor, though, I had this awful sense that as soon as the baby was pushed out of her womb, I was gonna be pushed out of my dad's heart completely. I didn't want to be at the hospital and I didn't want to be home alone either, so I got on my bike and just pedaled without thinking. It was only when I was three houses down from Jed's that I realized where I'd been headed. It was one of those perfect spring days you sometimes get in Oregon in March—clear blue skies and warm.

Jed was strumming an acoustic guitar on the porch. I didn't want him to see me, so I turned around and started to ride away. Then I heard him shout, "You're doing a roll by? That's just rude. Get up here and hang out for a while."

I dropped my bike against his front steps and climbed onto the porch. I must've looked awful, because Jed, who wasn't big on PDA, opened his arms and let me collapse into him. I cried so hard that I soaked the sleeve of his T-shirt, but he didn't seem to mind. He didn't act like I'd gone all basket case on him, either. He just stroked my head and kept saying "It's okay." Then he made us some coffee and came back out with two mugs and a cold washcloth for my face.

"Thanks," I said. "Stepmonster's having the baby."

Jed nodded. "I figured it was something like that."

"Things are gonna get so much worse. I don't know if I can take it."

I'd never told the band about my mom, but they seemed to understand something heavy had gone down. Not hard if you read between the lines of my song lyrics.

"You can take it," he said in a quiet voice.

"What makes you so sure? I mean, have you met me lately?"

Jed frowned slightly. "I know it's been rough. But I also know that you're strong."

"Yeah. That's me. Man of Steel. More like Girl of Tissue."

Jed shook his head. "You don't fool me. You're tough. Stronger than you even realize."

The next few hours were a blur of conversation and music. We took turns playing tracks from his record and CD collection, picking out songs that meant something to us. I played Jed the U2 and Bob Marley tunes I used to dance to with my mom. He played me Joan Armatrading and Frank Sinatra and things I'd never heard. The music got him talking and then he started telling me about summers in Massachusetts and fireflies.

"I've never seen a firefly," I said.

"For real?"

"'Fraid so. They don't have them out here in Oregon. We just have slugs."

"I've noticed. Hang on." He went back into his living room and pulled out a record. I could hear the needle scratch before the music came on. "This is American Music Club. Possibly the most melancholy band in the world. Seems fitting for tonight."

The song he'd picked was called "Firefly." It was the most achingly beautiful tune I'd ever heard. The lead singer started out inviting this girl to go outside with him and watch the fireflies darting around. His voice was so sorrowful, so full of longing. It was like he knew exactly what I was feeling. And when he played me "Firefly," Jed showed he understood too.

Then Jed sang the chorus right to me. "You're so pretty, baby, you're the prettiest thing I know. . . ." He was staring hard at me, and I swear, crazy as this sounds, I could feel a surge of electricity connecting us. I could hardly breathe. The song ended, the record stopped, and he was still looking at me, that smile in his eyes. I wanted to kiss him so bad. I moved toward him. And then *he* kissed me, light as a butterfly, right on my forehead. "You should probably go home," he whispered. "It's late."

I didn't want to go anywhere. I wanted to stay there and nuzzle my face into his neck and melt into him. But he wasn't offering that, and I didn't want to ruin the most romantic moment of my life.

So I left. And the next day Billy came home, and nobody could give two hoots about me at all. They were too busy cooing at the precious one, who was just a little eating, crying, pooping machine, as far as I could tell.

As for Jed, at the next band practice he was friendly and supportive like always, but it was as if that night had never happened. I was back to being his little sister. I assumed he'd forgotten all about it—until I got Dad's letter.

• • •

"Well, I think Miss Hemphill needs a special kind of encouragement," Sheriff bellowed. He went around with his rifle finger and stopped on Virginia, who was supposed to motivate the group by throwing out the harshest insults of all. "Miss Larson, you've been getting to know Miss Hemphill. What's behind her cool façade?"

Seeing V staring at me, her eyes hard and soft at the same time, I snapped back to the present. I knew what she was thinking. *Check your pride at the door. Get it over with. Give the dogs some meat to chew on or they'll really come after you.* And I knew she was right. I'd been to CT enough to see how it worked: Confess, cry, get out of the circle. But I was afraid that if I opened my mouth about anything, I was going to say things I didn't want anyone to know.

"You think you're so strong, with your punked-out hair and piercings. Except your hair's fading and your piercings are gone, so what are you now?" V screamed. "You're just an ordinary girl with some ink in her skin. You're nobody special." Her eyes searched my face, imploring me, and I understood what she was doing. She was throwing out softballs, laying a false scent for the dogs so they wouldn't catch me. I knew then that she was a friend.

"You think you're tough, but I've heard you cry," Tiffany said, jumping right in with her mightiest effort, which was in fact total BS. I didn't cry anymore. I gave Tiffany my most withering glare until she looked like *she* was going to cry. Brown-nosing wuss.

A few other girls threw out similarly lame comments but they failed to provoke. I just summoned some of that strength Jed had told me I had, and glared at everyone, daring them to mess with me. Without air a flame dies, and Sheriff didn't have the patience of some of the other counselors, who'd leave you in the ring for the whole hour. After ten minutes, I was pulled from the circle. It meant I could be moving down to Level Two, but I didn't care.

"Miss Wallace," Sheriff called. He had his rifle sight pointed at Martha, my overweight roommate, and I immediately felt my stomach lurch. No one got it in CT like the fat girls, and Sheriff, a man beyond clueless to the travails of being young, female, and overweight, was notoriously cruel. What's worse was that the whole room was amped up with unspent energy because I hadn't given up a thing. I knew Martha was going to take the beating I should have.

"Hey, fatty."

"Hey, lardass. Why do you eat so much?"

A couple of the girls were oinking like pigs. Sheriff was wearing a self-satisfied grin. He liked to say that you had to break before you could be fixed, but this was too much. Back at my school in Portland, this kind of name-calling would get you detention, but here it was called therapy. As the taunts rose into a chorus, Martha looked down, her face hidden behind her lank brown hair, and shuffled her feet in that way of hers, like she was an elephant trying to disappear behind a mouse. She stared at the floor while the chants continued. No one was even trying to pretend to be supportive here; there was none of the usual talk about using food to fight loneliness or to hide her beauty. Just two dozen girls taking out their body-image issues on the size-18 sucker in the mush pot. Like me, Martha didn't say anything, but she made the mistake of averting her gaze, the sign of defeat. Her back was to me, so I didn't know that she was crying until I saw the spatter of tears on the blue mat. Usually, once you let the waterworks go, you got a group hug, and pats on the back, and words of encouragement, but all Martha got was a Kleenex.

In the cafeteria that night, I sat next to Martha, who, like me, usually sat by herself. To my surprise, Bebe, Cassie, and V sat down next to us.

"I'm so sorry, Martha," I said. "It was my fault you got nailed today."

"No, it wasn't," V said. Her face was red with

anger. "Neither of you is at fault. It's this place's fault. Cruelty described as therapy. No wonder so many girls leave here more messed up than when they came."

"It was particularly brutal today, roomie," Bebe said. "And I thought my slut intervention was bad."

"Bad? You were havin' a grand ole time," Cassie said.

"It *was* kind of amusing. I mean, so what? Who isn't a slut these days?"

Martha just stared down at her plate of food, until she squeaked, "I don't get it."

"What?" I asked.

"I'm supposed to lose weight, but the only thing they have to eat is this stuff," she said pointing to her plate of breaded fish sticks, Tater Tots, and carrots so overboiled, they were dissolving into a blob under melted margarine. "If I eat this, I'll just get fatter, but if I don't eat it, I'll get written up," she whined, gesturing toward the clipboard-wielding counselors. And then she started sobbing.

Poor Martha. The food at Red Rock was positively vile. Everything was frozen and came in these industrial-sized metal tins: burgers of dubious meat origin, burritos, pizza, fish sticks, chicken nuggets, ice cream that didn't have cream in it, packaged cookies. The only fresh vegetable was iceberg lettuce salad with some scary old tomatoes. It was so disgusting that I ended up eating peanut butter and jelly sandwiches most days. But the girls on food watch didn't have the luxury of PB and Js. They were monitored all the time. If they ate too much, they got a black mark. If they didn't eat enough, they were suspected of starving themselves and got a black mark. Martha was supposed to lose weight, but in the catch-22 that was lame-ass Red Rock, she also had to clean her plate.

"Martha," V said in that sharp way of hers. "Don't cry. Don't let them see you weak. There are ways around everything in this place."

Martha looked up at her. "What ways?"

"Yeah," I asked. "What are these ways of yours?"

"Not here. Not now. But soon enough we'll have a little education for some of you newbies."

"Where?" I asked.

"Shh. Bebe will take care of you," V said. "Now let's scatter before we call more attention to ourselves." V stood up. "I'm glad you're starting to examine your food crutches, Martha," she said in an overly loud voice. Then she nodded her head, shot Martha a wink, and walked away.

Chapter 8

"Don't make a sound." Bebe was standing over me in her pajamas, with her hand over my mouth. I opened my eyes and she put her finger over her lips and mouthed, "Get up." She went over to Martha and did the same thing, except Martha jumped when she woke, and for a second it looked like Tiffany was up too. We all held our breath until Tiffany rolled back over and resumed snoring into her pile of stuffed animals.

Bebe led us out of our room and through the hallways to the T-junction where the residential units met the administrative offices. She pointed to the guard chair, which was empty, and an open utility closet where one of the goons was asleep on the floor. "He likes to nap between one and three, like clockwork, so we, my dears, have a small window of opportunity." It was a quarter past one.

"How'd you wake yourself up without an alarm clock?"

"I never went to sleep. I was just replaying my mom's old soap episodes in my mind. Always good for a laugh."

"What about the cameras?" I asked.

"They don't have them in the halls, and besides, they can't see crap when the lights are out."

She took us to a small office, empty save for V and Cassie, who were waiting for us there. We sat down in a circle on the floor and faced one another.

"Wow, how'd you know about this office? How'd ya get in?" Martha asked.

V held up a small silver key. "Secret number one," she said. "The pass key. It opens every door in the place."

"How did you manage to get that?" I asked.

"Our sneaky V stole it off the Sheriff's giant key ring," Cassie said.

"Let's just say I liberated it. Sheriff thinks he lost it.

And of course, they didn't want to pay to change all the locks," V said. "Now, let's get down to business."

"But what if we get caught?" Martha asked. "I don't want to get sent back to Level One."

"We won't get caught," V said, impatiently.

"How do you know that?" I asked.

"Look, I've been here for ages and I've followed this guard for months. He sleeps from one o'clock till three. You think I'd risk it if I thought we'd get nabbed? I'm on Level Six."

"Darlings, we're getting off to a bad start. Can we just begin?"

"I feel like we oughta have some kinda 'Hear ye, hear ye' announcement," Cassie said. "To make it all official."

"I see your point," V agreed. "Ladies, welcome to our new, what is it, a club? A clique?"

"Oh, let's call it a club," Martha said excitedly.

"A divinely fabulous . . ." Bebe said.

"Ultra-exclusive," I interrupted.

"Club," Martha crowed.

"Of the cuckoos!" Cassie added.

"Okay then. Welcome to the Divinely Fabulous Ultra-Exclusive Club of the Cuckoos," V said. "Now, it's time to get serious. After a year and half I've discovered ways to get around many of Red Rock's rules. I hate this place, and I'll do anything to fight it. I consider it my revolution from within."

V, Bebe, and Cassie went on to explain to Martha and me, among other things, how to sneak out letters by giving them to a sympathetic soon-to-be graduate or a trustworthy Level Fiver or Sixer before a town break. Failing that, one or two of the food-service guys could usually be trusted to smuggle a letter out.

"But you better check with us before you give a letter to anyone," V warned. "Red Rock gives the staff bonuses if they rat us out, but they also pay them crap the rest of the time, so some of the guys would rather stick it to them than earn twenty bucks for being a stool pigeon."

"Plus, I guarantee that after you've been here a while, you'll be able to get letters from non-family." Cassie gave me a reassuring wink.

"How?" I asked incredulously. "They read everything."

"Brit, darling, listen and learn," Bebe said. "You just have the person pretend to be your mother or brother or whoever. They read our outgoing mail, but they only skim the incoming stuff and if it says 'Love, Mom and Dad,' they'll buy it. They are so pathetically lazy, thank goodness."

"This is true, but you have to be careful and make sure to speak in code. Because if the letter gets tagged, you're screwed," V warned.

"What's the code?" I asked.

"Do you guys hear something?" Martha asked.

We all froze. "I swore I heard a voice," Martha whispered. V put her fingers to her lips. We all went silent. The only sound was our breathing and a clock ticking in the hall. I held my breath for extra insurance. I didn't want to get caught now that I was finally making friends.

After five minutes of silence, V went out for a look and saw the guard snoring away. "False alarm. We're fine."

"I'm sorry, I just thought . . ." Martha said.

"No, it's good to be vigilant." V gave Martha a reassuring nod.

"Can you get back to this code thing?" I asked, thinking of a person I'd like to get mail from.

"Right. Here's what we've done, and it's worked so far," V instructed us. "Discussions about the conditions at Red Rock should be veiled as worries about the health of Grandma, Grandpa, or Aunt Josephine or whoever. Declarations of affection or love from friends or boyfriends should be made through gushy descriptions of nice weather. Of course, the first contraband letter you mail should explain all the basic rules. After that it's up to you to come up with your own code. It's all a big wink-wink nudge-nudge thing. You'll know what you guys are talking about. Bebe has even managed to have some mail sex with her pool boy, all in code, and he doesn't speak English."

"His name is Pedro and yes he does," Bebe shot back.

"But don't get complacent, and don't get too clever or cute. You never know when they might single out a letter. That Clayton is smart, and if she smells a rat your goose is cooked."

"Ain't that a mixed metaphor?" Cassie asked.

V shot her a serious look. "If you get caught, bad diction will be the least of your troubles. Be careful. Be alert. And watch yourself here. Because they're watching us."

We all sat there in an ominous silence for a few minutes. V checked the hall clock. "It's almost three, so we should get back, but there's one more thing I want to tell you about. After you've been here a while, it's possible, under very particular conditions, to arrange a breakout for a few hours. Once you get town privileges, you can slip away for a while. Cassie's done it. This one girl, Deanna, even managed to disappear from a forced overnight hike and came back the next day with the staff none the wiser. That happened before I got here, but she's famous for it. We're miles from anything worth seeing, so breakouts are more of a last-ditch resort, when you just need to escape for a little while—and I don't think you new-bies should try just yet. But it makes you feel better knowing it's an option, doesn't it?" We all nodded. Martha raised her hand.

"Martha, we're not in class—what is it?"

"The food," she squeaked.

"Oh, of course. It's so simple I forgot," V said. "Socks."

"Huh?"

"Socks," Bebe elaborated. "Wear those big white sweat socks, the terribly unfashionable ones that bunch down your legs. And sneak your food into them. No one will ever notice, and you can dump the stuff in the yard."

Martha looked at her own thick white socks. "Why didn't I think of that?"

"We need to get back before the guard wakes up," V said. "So listen to this last bit. It's important. This place is not about fixing you. It's about warehousing you while your clueless parents are bilked out of thousands of dollars. Sheriff, Clayton, and the counselors do not care about us. And they don't want us to care about each other, so we've got to be sneaky. If we rely on each other, we won't go as nuts as our parents think we are." V put her arm into the circle.

"One for all and all for one?" Martha said, like a question. V nodded, and Martha put her hand in the circle.

"We, my dears, mustn't forget that we are the Divinely Fabulous Ultra-Exclusive Club of the Cuckoos," Bebe said, adding her hand.

"Sisters," said Cassie, putting her hand in.

"Sisters," I said, clapping my right hand on top of theirs. I felt the full strength of all of us together. "Sisters in Sanity."

Chapter 9

Dear Brit:

Happy Thanksgiving. Looking forward to a big turkey dinner at school? It'll be a quiet one at home. Your grandmother had hoped to join us, but her hip is hurting too much for the drive and she hates to fly. I'm sure if you were here, she would make the trip, though. She'd do anything for you.

We have received a few progress reports from the school. I understand your grades are up, which your mother and I are very happy about. The psychiatrist explains that you are making progress but *are also resistant to facing up to some things. I hope you will take advantage of this opportunity to work through your anger.*

We have also been told that you are now permitted to write letters. I look forward to hearing from you. Perhaps we will come for a visit after Christmas, if that is acceptable to your teachers.

I don't know what else to tell you. Rainy and dark here as usual. We've all been sick with bad colds for the last month. Tell me about where you are. While I know you don't want to be there, it must be a relief to have escaped the gray of Portland.

I love you.

Dad

P.S. I'll take a picture of Billy holding a drumstick for you!

Dear Dad:

I'm sure Thanksgiving will be fantastic this year. We'll all sit around in our warm cozy rooms and eat a home-cooked dinner and talk about how thankful we are for the constant supervision and the forced labor and the insults and the spying. Then we'll pig out on pumpkin pie and watch It's a Wonderful Life *on TV. The next day, we'll go to the mall to shop for presents.*

Hello? I know you think I'm the deluded one, but just what kind of place do you think you sent me to? I'm not supposed to tell you how awful Red Rock is, and you probably wouldn't believe me anyway.

Still, I don't understand why I'm here. The counselors seem to think the trauma of Mom has turned me into some wild, bad girl, but you and I know that's not true. I think the real reason I'm here is not because of you or me or what happened to Mom, but because of your wife. She obviously wants a family of three, and she's made it crystal clear that four's a crowd. Now she's brainwashed you into thinking the same thing.

As for Mom, I have been dealing with her issues for three years, and just because I don't feel like whining to some cold fish of a doctor (who, by the way, is not even a shrink—did you bother to check credentials?) doesn't mean I'm in denial. What am I supposed to do, wear a badge that says, "Hi, My Name's Brit and My Mom's a Schizo"? Because that's what would pass for progress *around here.*

I can't think too much about how I got here, because when I do I feel like I've been betrayed by you, and that makes me feel worse than everything else that's happened. Does Grandma know where you've sent me? I'm sure she'd be furious, but then again, you've never let anything she says change your mind.

You should come and visit. Maybe seeing this place up close would make you rethink your, or should I say, her, *decision.*

Brit.

P.S. The reason my grades have jumped is that the school here is completely remedial.

Billy could get A's here.
P.P.S. I'd take a year of Portland rain over
a sunny day in this hellhole.

"I see you haven't written your parents a letter," Clayton said to me, tapping her pen against a clipboard, something I swear she did to remind us all of the power she could wield with her little Bic. "Would you like to tell me why not? Most students are quite enthusiastic when they reach Level Four and are permitted to start communicating with family. Around the holidays, it's customary for students to send cards."

This was true. Red Rock even printed up these jolly cards with a picture of a bunch of smiling students in Santa hats and shorts for us to send home. They were total propaganda as far as I was concerned.

I had written my dad several versions of the same letter, but in the end I just tore them up and buried them in the quarry—in part because, as V warned me, outgoing letters would be scrutinized by staff, so you had to watch your attitude or they'd hold what you'd written against you in therapy. Clayton already acted as if she knew me better than I knew myself, and her smug attitude gave me the urge to smash things. There was no way I was going to let her read my mail to my dad, and I didn't think I could fake a casual, hey-how's-it-going letter to him either.

See, the thing was that in two months at Red Rock I'd had a lot of time to think, maybe too much time. I thought about Jed constantly; it was the only thing that made me feel good. But the rest of the time, I thought about Dad and Mom and me and, unfortunately, Stepmonster. And I thought about how much Dad had changed. As much as I wanted to pin this whole thing on Stepmonster, the sad reality was that Dad had gone along with her plan to send me away. If you had told me five years ago that my mellow, sweet father would dump his kid off at a boot camp, I would've told you that nothing, not even a gun to the head, could have pushed him to do such a thing.

"So why would he go along with it?" V asked me. The Sisters in Sanity had taken to meeting once a week in the empty office for our *real* therapy. It was the only time we could really talk about things that were bugging us, so I'd floated my theory to the group that Stepmonster hadn't acted alone.

"I don't know. He's just kind of a pushover, and she's a serious ball breaker."

"But you're his daughter. Surely if he didn't want you to be here, he could've mustered up some kind of opposition," Bebe said.

"Maybe he just doesn't want me around."

"Of course he wants you around!" Martha protested.

V arched her brow, Bebe narrowed her eyes, and Cassie guffawed.

"What?" Martha protested again.

"Darling, the obvious. If Dad wanted her around, why would she be here?" Bebe asked, turning back to me. "So, I think we've established that aside from some standard oppositional defiance disorder—and if you ask me, the sixteen year-old who doesn't exhibit those 'symptoms' is the one that's about to go Columbine—you're as sane as the next girl. So why did Daddy send you packing?"

"Maybe . . ." I started and then stopped.

"Maybe what?" V prompted.

"Maybe I'm just a reminder . . . of what happened to Mom." The minute the words came out, I knew that they were true. The Sisters knew that Mom had gone schizophrenic and disappeared, but I'd spared them the saga: the year-long ordeal of her personality change, the endless psychiatrists, Dad begging Mom to try different medications and even shock therapy, and then when she wouldn't, agonizing over whether or not to commit her. I didn't tell them about the last time we'd seen her, hanging out in back of Powell's bookstore, near the Dumpsters. She looked more like the ratty-looking homeless people you see all over Portland than like someone's mom. She didn't even seem to recognize me. And I didn't tell them how after that, I felt Dad starting to pull away from me.

"You did say that yah look a lot like your mom," Cassie said.

"Oh, well then," Bebe said, sweeping her hand through the air. "Mystery solved. And I can empathize. I'm certain my mom holds my striking resemblance to Husband Number Three—that would be my dad—against me. He was, after all, the only man who ever dumped her."

"No way. You look just like your mom," Martha said, blushing. "I used to watch her on *Lovers and Strangers*. She was the best. I can't believe she never got an Emmy."

"Why, thank you, Martha, but what has that got to do with anything?"

"Because Brit looks like her mom, so she's a constant reminder. That's why her dad let Stepmonster send her here."

"I don't know, Brit," V said. "This sounds a bit beyond the average Cinderella story. After all, Cinders' dad was dead, which explains her situation with the stepmom. But you have your dad, so the comparison doesn't quite work."

It occurred to me that the Sisters were only half right. Dad had probably sent me away because I reminded him of Mom, but after a few sessions with Clayton I had started to suspect that his reason may have been something even worse. What if he thought I was going to *end up* like her?

•   •   •

Clayton continued to grill me about my lack of epistolary enthusiasm. I just kept telling her that I wasn't very good at writing and that I figured Dad was getting lots of updates about me from the school. "He seems really happy about my grades and has mentioned coming for a visit," I told Clayton. "I'll just tell him everything then. But I love getting all the letters he sends me." She gave me a hard look. I never could tell if she bought my fake perkiness, but why else would she have advanced me to Level Four? V told me it was because, as an insurance-only stay, they had to make it seem like I was ready to go home after three months. Most people seemed to advance to Level Four quickly, but if your parents had deep pockets, you could fester at Red Rock for months.

Still, I wasn't *really* lying when I said I looked forward to some of Dad's letters. I'd snuck a letter out to Jed in November, just a quick note to say hi and explain my situation and ask about the band. I didn't want to go into much detail about my Red Rock experience, because part of me was really embarrassed about it. I wrote the letter to the whole band, even though I mailed it—or a graduate named Annemarie mailed it—to Jed's address. I also gave them a quick rundown of how the code worked, just in case they wanted to write back. I didn't want to put too much pressure on Jed to write back to little incarcerated me. I wasn't after his pity. But when I got my first letter after Thanksgiving, I knew it was from him. He had an old manual Underwood typewriter that he loved, and he'd even used it to type the address on the envelope.

Jed got the whole code thing so perfectly, which made a certain sense I guess, since songwriters are always writing in code. Most of his letter was about my "Uncle Claude," who plays violin in a chamber music ensemble. Claude had been sick of late, and the ensemble had been forced to play without him—the music was suffering. Then he told me about how the Portland skies were even rainier than usual—I wasn't entirely sure if that was a coded message that he missed me or if he was just being honest; you never knew with Oregon. But he ended the letter by saying that the winter was so long and dark that it made him yearn for summertime and fireflies. Which of course had my heart flipping.

Chapter 10

Every other week in the warmer months, Levels Three and Four got hauled on a ten-mile hike straight up into the hills. Sheriff liked to call these little expeditions "backcountry therapy."

"Backcountry therapy, my ass," Bebe said. "It's a death march."

"I hate these," Martha whined. "I thought they were supposed to stop in winter."

"Only when the snow comes, my dear. It's late this year. Poor us. God, it's hot for December. I'm sweating like a pig already. Ugh." Bebe checked her canteen. "I can't tell how much water I have left." For some reason, they gave us just one dinky water canteen, a

Baggie of trail mix, and an apple.

"So we'll sweat off our fat," Martha explained.

"No, darling, because suffering builds character," Bebe said. "If we're really hungry we're supposed to forage for food or something."

"I'd probably end up eating a poisonous mushroom," Martha insisted.

"Maybe you'd get lucky and get one of the magic kind," Bebe replied.

"Guys, it's the desert," I said. "They don't have mushrooms here. We'd have to eat cactus."

"Gross. Absolutely gross," Bebe huffed.

"Hey, you three," said Missy. She was a super-devoted Red Rocker who'd advanced to Level Four in practically a week. "Sheriff says to pick up the pace and stop the chatting."

"Yes *ma'am*," Bebe said, full of sarcasm.

Missy returned to the front of the pack and Bebe shook her head. "Stockholm Syndrome. So many girls get it. They come to love their captors."

"They're just brown-nosing to get out of here," I said.

"Maybe it starts that way, but they start to enjoy it. They even like these damn hikes. God, how much farther are we expected to go?" Bebe asked.

Bebe continued to bitch her way up and down the mountain, but the girl had logged enough hours on a Stairmaster to handle it. So could I. In Portland, I rode my old Schwinn cruiser around town. Plus, back in the day, I used to go hiking with Mom and Dad through Forest Park. Stepmonster, of course, preferred to spend weekends at the mall. I secretly enjoyed the death march, in part because I knew how much she would have hated it.

Martha, on the other hand, had a tough time of it. "I can't breathe," she cried through her wheezes. "I'm never gonna make it."

"You always say that, dear, and you always make it," Bebe said.

"Just one foot in front of the other," I encouraged her.

"But my feet are killing me."

"Don't think about that. Look at the scenery," I said. It was pretty otherworldly—with red rock, red clay, and weird coffin-shaped boulders jutting out everywhere. It looked like Mars.

"I don't want to look at the scenery," Martha moaned. "I don't want to be here at all. I want to be back home in Ohio, walking through a nice park to have a picnic."

"Picnic. Fab idea. What are we having?" Bebe asked.

"Huh?"

"What's on the menu for the picnic?" Bebe asked again.

Martha fell silent for a while, but then she piped up: "My mom's chicken-salad sandwiches. They're the best. Not too mayonnaise-y."

"What else?" I asked, glad to distract her.

"My mom makes these twice-baked potatoes with cheese and sour cream. They're supposed to be eaten hot, but they taste even better cold. Then we'll have some cut-up carrots and celery to be healthy. And watermelon. And ice-cold lemonade. The homemade kind, not the powdery stuff."

"What about dessert?" I asked.

Martha pondered that for a second. "Can we have two choices?"

"It's your picnic, darling. We can have as many as you want," Bebe said.

"Icebox cake. It's this thing my grandma used to make. Chocolate biscuits all crunched up with whipped cream and chocolate sauce, and then frozen. It's like an airy ice-cream cake that doesn't melt all over."

Bebe and I were both salivating now. "What's the other option?" I asked.

"Strawberry shortcake. Little individual ones, really thin, with fat strawberries that we picked ourselves, and fresh whipped cream."

"Oh, stop it Marth," I said. "This is torturous, worse than the hike."

"I know, I'm hungrier than ever," Martha said. But she was also almost at the summit. When we sat down to eat our apples and trail mix we tried to pretend they were Martha's dream picnic. It almost worked.

Two weeks later, we had the first snowfall of the season. "Thank God," Martha said, looking at the falling flakes. "No more backcountry therapy."

I wished group therapy would be over for the season, too. I came to dread the sessions almost as much as my meetings with Clayton. I had tried to fly under the radar for the first few months, and it sort of worked. During the CT sessions, I'd only been put in the hot seat that one time with Sheriff. But after Thanksgiving, all of a sudden my honeymoon was over. Now it was like I was the counselor's pet project. I wound up in the CT circle twice in one week, and twice they couldn't get me to cry, even when they mentioned my mom. Some of the Stockholm-Syndrome girls were starting to get nasty with me too, constantly harping on me about not working my program. As if it was any of their business.

Plus, now that the weather was cooler, the counselors patrolled the yard to keep warm, and that kind of ruined the joy of the quarry. We couldn't talk as much, and we were separated a lot more. And they just got randomly nasty and controlling for no reason. I happen to have a small bladder and had to pee a lot because I drink lots of water when I'm building walls. When it was hot, we got quarry bathroom breaks once an hour, but now that it was cold, we were only permitted to go every two hours. Most of the time, when I raised my hand, they let me go, but one day, one of the goons refused to let me. "I think you use your bladder as a form of control," he told me. Yeah, to control my pee. I was about to wet my pants so I waited for him to pass and squatted behind a rock.

A dorky Level Four chick named Jenny caught me and started screaming, "Oh, disgusting. She's *going* on the ground!"

God, you would've thought I'd peed on someone. I got pulled from the quarry and hauled straight into Clayton's office. She was livid, turning shades of red.

"Your continual defiance is getting tiresome," she said coldly.

"*I'm* not defiant. My *bladder* is. It's got a mind of its own," I said.

That remark turned out to be a little too smartass. Clayton turned purple. "I thought I told you to stay away from Miss Larson."

"What does V have to do with my bladder?" I gave Clayton my best are-you-nuts face.

"This kind of insubordination has her fingerprints all over it."

For some reason, this made me furious, and now I was the one turning purple. "I'm my own person, Dr. Clayton, as much as you people here want to change that. I can be insubordinate all on my own."

"I see that you can, Brit. And trust me, we'll be working on that."

I expected to be demoted to Level Three right there and then, but Clayton had other plans for me. They sent really bad girls to Red Rock's version of a naughty chair. It was a small hut, next to the quarry, with a dirt floor and nothing much else. For three days, instead of working the quarry, I had to sit on my ass and not move, not talk, not eat, and not pee for four hours straight. I know it was meant to be a kind of torture, but aside from my cold feet and my numb butt I kind of enjoyed the solitude. I even felt triumphant. They couldn't break me so easily.

But Clayton wasn't through with me yet. A few mornings later, I got my runny oatmeal from the cafeteria and went to sit down next to V. She shook her head at me. At first I thought it was the reemergence of her Jekyll and Hyde personality, but later, at the quarry, the counselors immediately separated us, and I got the sense that something bigger was going on. Bebe filled me in that night. V had been called into Clayton's office and berated for exerting her bad influence not just on me, but on Martha and Bebe as well. She was stripped of much of her Level Six authority (no more leading CT sessions, to V's relief) and was warned to keep her paws off of us—or say hello to Level Five.

"It appears the party is over, darlings," Bebe whispered from her bunk.

"What party?" Tiffany asked. "You guys aren't throwing a party or anything? If you get me in trouble, I swear, I'll tell."

"There's no party, and if there were, rest assured, you wouldn't be invited," Bebe replied, making me grateful, not for the first time, that I was on her good side. Sometimes she could be such a bitch.

So, that was the end of the Sisters in Sanity—at least the public face. From then on, we had to lay low, keep our friendship more secret. Which was the most lame-ass thing I'd ever heard of. What kind of messed-up place didn't want you to have friends, to have any kind of good time? What kind of place wanted you to be lonely, sad, and miserable—all in the name of therapy?

Chapter 11

As Christmas approached, none of us was feeling too merry. First we had the Sisters crackdown. And then it was like, instead of the holidays infusing the staff with some good cheer, it made them more surly. Maybe they thought a little Christmas joy would undo all the tough love they'd been smothering us with. They paid lip service to the holidays by making us decorate the halls, but that was about it. We didn't get any break in our schedule. No party, no tree.

The anti-Christmas got me thinking about last year. Clod had played a sold-out day-after show at the X-Ray. When we'd finished our set, we walked down to the riverfront to exchange our presents: I'd found

Erik a Ramones-emblazoned cigarette lighter, Denise a beaded handbag, and Jed a pulp edition of the Jim Thompson book *Pop 1280*. My gift made Jed so happy that he gave me a kiss, somewhere between the mouth and the cheek. That had me buzzing for hours. And later on, when I started shivering from the cold, he pulled me close to warm me up. It was probably more a friendly thing than anything romantic, but I still felt all oozy inside and wanted to stay there forever.

There'd be none of that this year. Only Level Five and Six girls were allowed to receive presents from home. The rest of us could only get cards. Exchanging presents among ourselves? Not allowed either. Not that we had anything to give: The staff had refused our request for a Christmas-shopping field trip.

It was V's idea to exchange presents anyhow. "We obviously can't give traditional presents," she said the week before Christmas. She'd managed to sneak up to Bebe and me on the cafeteria line. "Clearly that's not an option here, or I'd give you all cashmere socks. But let's all try to come up with something. I'll tell Cassie; you let Martha know. Then if the coast is clear, we can sneak away to our usual place on Christmas Eve for a private party."

Right when V said that, I knew what my present to her would be, and thanks to Clayton, I'd already started it. During all those empty hours in the Naughty Hut, I'd worked on it and the time had slipped by. I was excited about sharing my project with the Sisters, but nervous, too, that they wouldn't like it. I was also pretty curious to see what they'd "get" me. Nervous, eager, and curious—kind of like a kid the night before Christmas.

•   •   •

"Well, darlings, it's not quite a day at the Peninsula, but it will have to do," Bebe said, spreading out a bunch of fancy moisturizers, bath salts, makeup, and hair-product samples. V had worried that Christmas Eve would be a risky time to sneak out, but half the staff was away, and the rest, we figured, were getting hammered.

"Martha, you strike me as a Kiehl's girl," she said, giving her some cucumber lotion. "Brit, you are so M·A·C," she said, presenting me with a tube of Lipglass. "You'll love it—it feels like liquid sexiness.

V, your hair's getting a little unchunky, so this ought to help," she said, handing over some Bed Head samples. "And finally, Cassie, some lavender oil for you. It's nice-smelling, but not too much like perfume. I know you don't do the girlie thing."

"Wow," Martha said. "Where'd you get all this stuff?"

"You forget that Mother is a spa whore. Day spas and salons are practically her hobby. She's been sending me this crap ever since I got to Level Four. So Merry Christmas, my dears. Be beautiful. Who's next?"

"Gee, I feel like mine's a lump of coal compared to Bebe's beauty bounty," Cassie said.

"Oh please, this was nothing," Bebe said. "Just my mother's sloppy seconds. What do you have for us, as it seems Santa has forsaken us this year?"

"Christmas chocolate," Cassie exclaimed, pulling out a giant Hershey bar. We all started drooling.

"Cass, how did you score that?" V asked.

"My folks brought it for me."

"But that visit was months ago."

"In September, but I'm sure it's still good. Chocolate lasts forever, don't it?"

"Even antique chocolate would do," I said. "But how could you hang on to a Hershey Bar for three months? I'd have decimated it ages ago."

"I wanted to save it . . . for somethin' special . . . like this."

"Darling, how touching," Bebe said.

"Can we eat it now?" Martha begged.

"Do pigs like dirt?" Cassie asked.

"God, I've no idea," Bebe admitted. We all laughed.

"Just a sayin', Bebe. Dig in, girls." Cassie peeled off the brown wrapper, and we were instantly intoxicated by the smell of sweet, chocolatey goodness.

"Now this is bliss," V said, biting into a piece. "Okay, Martha, you're next."

"Mine is sort of silly. I didn't really know what to give."

"Martha darling, your self-deprecation is getting old."

"Huh?"

"Bebe means stop worrying about it," I said. "I'm sure we'll love it."

"Okay, but they're not very good. I didn't have charcoals or anything. I had to use pencil. But here."

Martha pulled four postcard-sized pieces of cardboard out of her pocket. They were drawings of each of us, really good drawings that made us look like the girls we once were. Except in Martha's rendition, we were superheroes. She drew me with a mane of wildly colored hair, wielding a flaming guitar like a weapon. She'd conjured Bebe like an old thirties movie star, holding a magic wand in her hand. She'd made V an Amazonian giant, towering over the world, with one high-heeled boot about to smash an ugly building that looked not unlike Red Rock. Cassie had bulging muscles under a DON'T MESS WITH TEXAS T-shirt and was juggling bricks. We all had capes, and on the bottom of each card Martha had written, "Sisters in Sanity: Superhero Series."

"Because you guys are—you're like my heroes," Martha said.

Nobody said anything for a second, and we all got a little misty.

"Darling," Bebe said. "Who knew you were such an artist?"

"These are great," Cassie said.

"Really?" Martha asked, her eyes shining.

"Let's raise our chocolate to Martha," V said.

"Thanks, Martha." I gave her a hug.

"You three outdid yourselves. And now I'm the one feeling a little silly. I'm afraid my present will be a little anticlimactic," V said.

"Come on, V. We don't even need a gift from you. *You're* the reason we're all here," I reminded her. "That's the biggest gift."

V's eyebrows arched up. "Wrong, Brit. We're all here because of one another. We're in this together."

"Now who's full of false modesty?" I asked. "You're the one who gives all the good advice, teaches us how to get around, and makes this place bearable!"

"That's sweet of you to say, Cinders, and it falls in line with my gift. On my last field trip into town, I met these women at the movies. They cornered me in the bathroom, actually. Turns out they used to be counselors here, but unlike the rest of the ghouls, these two had a conscience. One got fired for complaining about how we were treated, and then the other quit in protest. They live in St. George and they share our hatred of Red Rock. They told me that if I ever needed help escaping for the night, or getting ahold of someone on the outside, they'd try to arrange it. So, my gift to you is an IOU. I promise to arrange a prison break for each one of you. I'm totally serious. This is a real IOU, not one of those fake coupons good for doing dishes that you used to give your parents on their anniversary."

"V, it's too dangerous," Martha said.

V shrugged her shoulders. "I like to live on the edge."

"I'll say one thing, sister," Cassie added. "You got balls."

"Cassie darling, don't you mean she has eggs?" Bebe asked. "You of all people should know better."

"Oh, shut your trap," Cassie said affectionately.

Then they turned to me, and I was suddenly more nervous than I'd been onstage at my first gig. I took a deep breath.

"All right. First you have to imagine this with guitars, two of them, both acoustic, kind of echoey, like Nirvana unplugged. And then it goes from G to D to A minor, kind of like this." I hummed the chords.

"You wrote us a song?" V asked. I nodded, and she flashed her completely disarming smile my way.

"So, as I was saying, it kind of goes like this, and then it'll have a low bass and a really soft drumbeat.

Very Beck-in-his-quiet-phase-sounding."

"Brit, just sing," V said.

And so I did.

> There are monsters all around us
> They can be so hard to see
> They don't have fangs, no blood-
>   soaked claws
> They look like you and me.
>
> But we're not defenseless
> We're no damsels in distress
> Together we can fend off the attack
> All we gotta do is watch our backs.
>
> Your body is beautiful how it is
> Who you love is nobody's business
> We all contemplate life and death
> It's the poet who gives these thoughts
>   breath.
>
> The monster is strong, don't be
>   mistaken
> It thrives on fear—keeps us isolated

But together we can fend off its attack
All we gotta do is watch our backs.

In your darkest hour
When the fight's made you weary
When you think you've lost your
*   power*
When you can't see clearly
When you're ready to surrender
Give in to the black
Look over your shoulder
I've got your back.

We ended the first annual Divinely Fabulous Ultra-Exclusive Club of the Cuckoos Christmas party hugging each other with misty eyes. Then we clinked imaginary glasses of eggnog and sang "I've got your back." V declared it was our new theme song.

The next morning, when it was Christmas for real, the counselors distributed our holiday cards from home. I got three, one from my grandma and two from my dad. One had a bunch of reindeer sitting around a giant candy cane and it was from the whole family; the other was of Santa on a Harley-Davidson in a biker outfit and just said, "Be merry, Firefly." When the day was over, I couldn't help thinking that while this definitely ranked as one of the worst Christmases of my life, in a weird way, it was also one of the best.

Chapter 12

"Why do you think your father sent you here, Brit?" Clayton asked me. It was the middle of January, and the skies had turned white with clouds and the wind howled icy drafts up and down the building. It was truly dreary.

"Because my stepmother wanted me out of the way."

"Don't you think that excuse is a little too convenient? Life's not a fairy tale." She droned on. Of course, this is also what the Sisters had been saying, but I wasn't about to discuss that with Clayton. That was the maddening thing about her. I mean, Sheriff could be gruff and harsh, but like most people at Red Rock, he didn't have the patience to stick with it. But with Clayton it was like my refusal to get with her program was some kind of personal affront. Whenever I came to her dank little office, she made a big show of going through my file and pursing her lips to show me how much she disapproved. Then she'd say something like, "You might think your defiant attitude is something to be proud of, but truly, it's not. It's just a sign of your denial." Blah blah-blah blah. And you couldn't just tune Clayton out. She wasn't dumb, and she knew how to find your sore spots. After a few months with no great breakthrough for me, she started hitting mine big-time.

"Your father would not have sent you here had he not wanted you to get some help."

"So you keep saying."

"Why won't you talk to me about your mother?"

"You know, Dr. Clayton. I'm sure my dad has told you the whole story. And besides, it's not like I haven't thought about my mom before. I've had three years to work through the situation with my mom, and talking to you isn't going to change anything."

She sighed again and shook her head. "Are you angry at your father for sending you here?"

"No, I'm grateful. I love it."

She scribbled some notes. Clayton was no fan of sarcasm. "You don't trust me much, do you?" she asked.

I shrugged.

"Why not?"

This question always slayed me. In spite of their nasty tactics, Red Rock's counselors were always asking why we didn't trust them. For once, I decided to tell the truth. I looked into Clayton's pinched-up face and let loose: "Because this is not the after-school-special version of life, in which I open up to you and you calm my fears and I leave here fixed. What you want, what Red Rock wants, is to turn me into some obedient automaton, who'll never disagree with my stepmother, talk out of line to Dad, or do 'rebellious' stuff like play music or dye my hair. What you don't get, what my Dad doesn't seem to get any-more, is that I'm not rebellious at all. I was raised this way. 'Always march to your own drummer,' my mom used to tell me. Those were her words to live by. So it's not like *I* switched course. *Everyone else* did. That's why I'm here."

When I stopped talking, I was breathing hard. I expected Clayton to be moved, pissed off at least, but judging by her blasé expression, I may as well have been speaking Swahili.

"Are you angry at your father for divorcing your mother?"

I slumped back in my seat, suddenly exhausted by her questions. I understood why Dad divorced Mom, because even though she was still out there somewhere, she was gone, and the doctors said that she wasn't coming back—not the way she used to be anyhow. If Mom had died, I would've wanted Dad to get on with his life, not to spend his days moping for her, and I guess it was kind of like she *had* died. But another part of me wondered how he could move on without her.

"Why wasn't your mother committed?" Clayton asked.

I shrugged again. Truth was, Dad was the only one who could legally do it, and he didn't have the stomach for it. Grandma used to plead with him, crying,

"Please, please, she's my little girl." Dad would cry back, "I can't." He'd fallen in love with Mom's free spirit, and he couldn't bring himself to clip her wings. And in case anyone thinks I'm in denial, it's not lost on me that while my Dad couldn't commit my totally nutso mom—even with everyone begging him to—all it took was a little nudging from Stepmonster for him to lock me up. But I wasn't about to share *that* with Clayton. We'd had enough "honesty" for one day. In fact, I'd had enough of Clayton for one day too. I needed to get away from her, even if I had to burn a bridge to do it.

"You know, if you're so interested in my dad, maybe you should shrink his head. Oh, but you're not really a shrink, are you? Just play one on TV, huh."

Clayton snapped my file shut and licked her pale, thin lips. We still had fifteen minutes left in the session, but she stood up. My little jibe had worked. It had also cost me a level. "I'm moving you back to down to Level Three. I'm disappointed in you. Very disappointed." She stared at me with her best look of disapproval, trying to gauge how upset I was. Whatever. Level Four, Level Three—the only difference was I couldn't wear makeup, which I didn't anyway. And I couldn't talk on the phone, which was just as well because my weekly five minutes with Dad were really awkward. Neither of us knew what to say, and half the time, Dad put a babbling Billy on the line to fill the silence.

Demotion, promotion, it didn't seem to matter. Now that I'd passed the three-month mark, I knew I wasn't getting out of Red Rock soon. I got up to leave, but before I was out the door, Clayton went in for the kill. "Sooner or later, you're going to have to talk about your mother, about the ways in which her nature mirrors your own."

"What are you talking about?" I screamed, unable to control myself any longer. "My mom didn't just stay out too late because she was playing in a band or because she didn't like her stepmother! She was sleeping in parks, hiding from imaginary people she thought were trying to kill her. My mom got sick, like with cancer, but in her head. She has a mental illness, not a character defect. And I'll never talk about her with you. *Never!*"

I ran back to my room and threw myself on the

bed, sobbing uncontrollably for my mom and for everything else I'd lost. I didn't go to dinner, and none of the counselors forced me to go, either. After all, I was crying. They liked it when you cried.

• • •

"Darling, darling, what is it?" Bebe asked. It was after lights-out, and I had my head jammed into my pillow, which was soaked with tears.

"Brit, why are you so upset? You're scaring me," Martha said.

"It's lights-out. Can you all be quiet? Otherwise we're going to get in trouble," Tiffany whined.

"Not as much trouble as you're in if you don't butt out and shut your trap, Tiffany," Bebe snarled.

"You guys are so nasty. I swear I'm going to tell Clayton."

"You do that and you'll regret the day you were born," Martha said in an uncharacteristic show of toughness. It would've made me smile if I hadn't felt so awful.

"Whatever," Tiffany said.

"Brit, tell us what happened," Martha begged.

I couldn't talk. Didn't want to say anything. Bebe and Martha just leaned over my bed, ignoring Tiffany's dramatic sighs. Martha stroked my arm and Bebe whispered "Don't cry, sweetie," until I finally fell asleep.

Chapter 13

"This girl needs some cheering," said V, who, along with Cassie, Bebe, and Martha, was standing over me at lunch. It had been two days since the horrible session with Clayton, and I was still feeling kind of wrecked by it.

"You guys, don't sit here. We'll pay for it," I said.

"We can live dangerously just this once," V said, motioning to the others. "Sit down."

They sat down, all looking at me with a strange mix of worry and concern, which was nice but made me feel like a lab rat. Then they looked at one another and smiled.

"What? What's going on?"

"So listen, Cinderella, I have some good news," Bebe said.

"You're going home?"

"Not quite, darling, but nice of you to think it. No, this pertains to you, all of us really. We have a fairy godmother, you see. A most unlikely one," Bebe said.

"Who?"

"My mother, of course. She has found her calling, hosting a cable show all about beauty spas. Could it be *more* perfect? Anyhow, as it turns out, there are several chichi spas in the area. Something about the red clay being therapeutic. Mother's coming here to film them. So guess who's getting a day at the spa?"

"You?" I said.

"Well, of course me, darling. But also you four."

"No way," I said. "They'll never let us go. Especially now, when they're keeping such an eye on us. And I just got demoted, remember?"

"Ahh, you underestimate the power of celebrity, even washed-up C-list celebrity. Mother has promised to grant an audience with the staff, and the counselors are all peeing themselves with glee. Even Sheriff asked if he could get an autographed picture. I had my mother specially request your presence. Trust me, they'll do what she asks. All you need is permission from your own parents to go."

"Me at a girlie spa," Cassie said. "My parents are gonna faint from joy."

"Yeah, all I have to do is tell my parents that I'm getting an anti-cellulite treatment," Martha said.

"Even if they did let me go, how am I gonna get permission? I'm demoted, remember. Level Three. No phone calls. Besides, my dad's probably pissed that I'm not progressing fast enough."

"She's coming in ten days. Write a letter today. And make it a good one, full of introspection. At the end, tug on his heartstrings and ask if you can go. If you mail the letter right away, your dad will have time to call in with permission."

"Unless Stepmonster reads the letter first. But even if Dad says yes, I can't see Clayton agreeing."

"Clayton doesn't make the final decisions on such things, my dear. The Sheriff does. And he's gaga for Mother."

"Okay, I'll write to him. Maybe as an added incentive, I'll tell him I really want to cut out my streaks." This wasn't entirely untrue. In the months since I'd been at Red Rock, the magenta had faded to a rather putrid shade of orange and my roots were coming in under the black.

"Speaking of which, I'm in desperate need of a cut," V said. Her once-choppy locks were also looking a little tired.

"That reminds me. I've always wondered where you got such a cool haircut out here. Did they let you go to a salon in town or something?"

V and Bebe laughed.

"You're sweet, Brit. But if my hair turned out cool, it was purely accidental. I had really long hair when I got here, but I shaved it all off."

"What?"

"I used the electric razors they give us."

"Wow, that's so punk rock."

"You don't have the lock on rebellion, you know." V grinned at me in that snarky way of hers, which by now I'd learned was totally affectionate.

"Ladies, can we get back to the subject at hand? A day out. A day of beauty. It's going to be divine. You know what they say. 'Look good, feel good.'"

You wouldn't guess it to look at me, but I'm a sucker for pampering and stuff. Mom and I used to have do-it-yourself beauty days at home. But I'd never been to a real spa. And the thought of a day out gave me a burst of energy. All of us were really excited. Every time we passed one another in the hall, we'd call out, "Look good, feel good," and laugh. Even the staff let us have our joke. Everyone was looking forward to the pending arrival of Marguerite Howarth, aka Ellis Hardaway, the resident villain on *Lovers and Strangers* for fifteen years before she was murdered by her half sister. No one even dared call Bebe "Rodeo Drive" anymore, for fear of offending her, I guess, and being excluded from meeting her mom. And Bebe herself seemed the most excited of all.

"I can't wait for you to meet Mother," she gushed. "She's a major diva and a bit of a head case, don't get me wrong. All actors are. But she's a lot of fun, and she will simply adore you all."

• • •

As it turned out, we would all have to wait a bit longer to meet Marguerite. Two days before our big spa trip, she called Bebe to say she had just gotten a small role in a made-for-TV movie about figure skaters and wouldn't be coming to Utah after all.

"She wanted me to tell you how sorry she was. And she'll send some *samples*," Bebe said, practically spitting out her words.

"I'm so bummed. I wanted to meet her," Martha lamented. V shot Martha her harshest arched eyebrow, shutting Martha up.

"I'm so sorry, Bebe," I said. "Parents. They are clueless."

"Unbelievable," added V. "And they wonder why we're a little out of whack."

"Yeah," I said, "maybe they should send all our parents to boot camp."

"I can just see fancy Ellis Hardaway workin' the brick pile," Cassie said.

Even Bebe had to chuckle at the thought of that.

• • •

A couple days later, V sidled up next to me while I was building a wall. Though Clayton kept trying to separate us, V bristled at being told what to do, so every now and then she'd wend her way over to visit me. "It's tragic that Bebe's mom bailed, but she should have known better. We all should've," she said. "Parental visits are a rarity here. There's even something in the brochure about how the therapy works best when the troubled girl is removed from her familiar context completely."

"The better to make you miserable. But I thought your mom came," I said.

"She swung by once when I hit Level Five for the first time. She was at some conference in Vegas, so she had to come."

"What about your dad?"

"He works for the United Nations. As a diplomat. He travels a lot. Anyhow, Mom did visit, but she couldn't do that now. Not since Alex."

"Who's Alex?"

"Where would you get your gossip if it weren't for me?"

"Dunno. I'd be lost, I guess."

"Right. Alex was just some girl here. She hated it as much as we all do. And she wrote her parents all these letters about how awful it was, how dirty it was, how the therapists were all bogus. The only difference was that Alex's parents believed her. Can you imagine?"

"Crazy concept. Trusting your child."

"I know. Insane. Anyhow, her parents came by for a surprise visit. It was summer and blazing out, and we were all in the quarry in the middle of the day. The place was a dump as usual. Her father freaked out right there. He was screaming about suing this place for malpractice. They took Alex home that day."

"I wish that would happen to me."

"It's the ultimate fantasy. But now drop-in visits are pretty much banned. Parents have to sign a contract when they enroll you, promising to abide by the 'therapeutic guidelines' and swearing not to sue if you get killed in Red Rock's care."

"No way."

"That's not the exact wording. But there is a contract, and it says you can't visit without prior permission."

"How is it that you know everything?"

V smiled mysteriously. "I have my ways," she said, and then before I could ask her about those ways, she was on the other side of the quarry.

•   •   •

There were parental visits, of course. I mean most parents did want to see their offspring now and again. And family visits were a good "motivator." It was amazing how after a few months at Red Rock, even girls who had terrible relationships with their parents were dying to see them. So Red Rock set up pre-arranged visits, called them therapy, and then charged extra for them. "Family Intensives" were held four times a year at a nearby hotel. Parents hardly even saw the school—they came by for an hour-long tour and a meal. The joke of it was, the week before the visits, we were all taken off the quarry and turned into maids, scrubbing the dingy halls, bleaching the skanky bathrooms. And when the parents came for lunch, the meal was catered. Not a very realistic view of life at Red Rock.

Of the five of us, only Cassie's parents had come to one of the meetings, which Cassie said wasn't too bad. One perk of Family Intensives was that you got to stay at the hotel where they held the thing, which meant a whole weekend of TV and swimming pools.

"And TGI Friday's. I had potato skins for dinner every day," Cassie said.

We had just finished a group therapy session, and

the counselors announced which girls would be on the list for the next Family Intensive a few weeks later in March. Naturally, none of us was included, and Cassie was trying to make us feel better.

"The therapy part was the pits. All the parents sittin' around gettin' teary about how messed up we are and how glad they are that we're on the road to recovery."

"And let me guess, there wasn't any talk of how your parents might have contributed to any of your problems, and I'll bet none of you guys had the guts to bring that up anyhow," Bebe said. She was still pretty bitter about Marguerite's aborted visit.

"Well now, what was I s'posed to do? Blame my folks? Come on, they've darn near sold the farm tryin' to fix me."

"You live on a farm?" Bebe asked snidely.

"It's just an expression," Cassie said, looking wounded.

Cassie's parents had gone haywire trying to degayify her. After a family vacation in Corpus Christi, when they caught Cassie kissing a surfer girl, they sent her to some gender dysphoria expert they'd read about online, only she turned out to be a shrink who mostly worked with transsexuals, so then they switched to a therapist who specialized in "fixing" gay kids, and it was that guy who referred them to Red Rock.

"Why not blame your parents?" Bebe asked. "Mom didn't give you enough attention. Dad didn't give you enough love and now you're a big ole lesbian."

"That ain't true," Cassie said. "I don't even know that I'm gay. I think I'm bi, but if you think about it, so's everyone. We're just tryin' to figure things out."

"Not me, darling. I don't go for girls. And might I remind you that you got caught making out with some surfer girl? I'd say that qualifies you as a dyke."

"And you got caught doin' lord knows what with your pool boy, but that doesn't make you a slut in my book."

"You're right. All the *other* guys I've done, that qualifies me as a slut."

"Bebe, stop it," I said.

"Oh please, not you too, Cinders. You're not going to turn yourself into a doormat for these drones."

"No, I'm not," I insisted. "And neither is Cassie.

And just because you're pissed off at your mom doesn't give you the right to dump on everyone else or to tell Cassie that she's gay or not gay."

Bebe gasped as if I'd hit a nerve. "I have the right to say what I think," she said.

"What are you, ten?" I knew Bebe was bummed, but I couldn't stand to watch her take it out on Cassie.

"Oh piss off, Miss Bad Girl." Bebe stared me down as if only *she* could see the real me. "You think you're such a rebel," she said, "but you're really just a goody-two-shoes."

"I don't have to prove anything to you," I said, fuming.

"That's all you do—*try to prove stuff*," she shot back.

"Spare me the cheap psychobabble," I said, rolling my eyes. "I get enough of that around here."

"Well maybe you need some more."

"No, maybe you do. Look, Bebe, I know you're angry, but enough with the bitchiness already," I said. "We are all *so* over it."

"Well, I guess my fifteen minutes of sympathy are up," she said sarcastically. "Fine. Whatever. Just you wait until it's your dad that cancels on you. Oh, but that probably won't happen because he doesn't even want to see you in the first place, does he?"

"Bebe darling?"

"What?" she snapped.

"Go to hell."

Bebe and I iced each other that night and all the next day. I was furious with her, but I also knew I had to let it go. When you're surrounded by enemies, you can't really afford to hold grudges against your friends. Bebe realized the same thing. Two mornings later I found another of her notes stuck inside my shirt pocket.

I'm a bitch. I'm an idiot. I'm sorry.
Forgive me? ☺ *BB*

I did, of course. I knew how frustration could build until you were ready to explode. Sometimes you just had to lash out at someone, and it was safer if we did that to each other. I also knew that what Bebe said wasn't really about me or meant to hurt me. But her words hit home. In his letters, Dad *did* keep promising to visit. He was all gung ho, talking about making it a family trip with Billy and the Stepmonster, and while I had no desire to see her, I still wanted Dad to prove me wrong and show up. Although, having sunk down to Level Three, I wasn't really in any position to have a family visit anyway. Despite the fact that I had been trying to "work my program." Sort of.

V kept telling me to fake it, that all I had to do was open up in CT. It didn't matter if what I was opening up about was total crap. So I invented sob stories about how alienated I was at school, how mean the other kids were to me. I even squeezed out a tear in one session. The counselors were impressed with my bravery and—get this—honesty. I thought for sure I was going back to Level Four, but I must have really pissed Clayton off, because even with all my feigned progress, I remained stuck on Level Three. I wasn't going to see Dad in March and the next Family Intensive wasn't until June—*June!* It was starting to look like was I going to be stuck at Red Rock for the summer. And what if they made me stay for my senior year?

That was one of the worst things about it, the not knowing. If you murder someone and go to jail, you're allowed visitors, and you have a specific sentence, but the Sisters and I didn't get those rights.

After three months passed and I realized I wasn't one of the insurance-only girls, it was a constant guessing game of trying to figure out when I'd be released. I was beginning to wonder if I'd be living at Red Rock until my eighteenth birthday. The thought of that thoroughly depressed me—which was ironic, and pathetic. I was always a pretty high-spirited person. I got sad, of course, especially when Mom started to melt down, but I was engaged in my world. It wasn't until Red Rock that I started feeling empty, tired, and angry most of the time. There were some days when I just wished I could disappear from the world. So not only did I have no idea *when* I'd be getting back to my real life, I had no idea *who* I'd be when that happened.

Chapter 14

Dear Brit:

How are you? How is school? I hope you are working very hard and getting good grades. Portland is as rainy and gloomy as ever. I sure wish I could be somewhere nice and warm and sunny.

I wanted to give you some very exciting news about your Uncle Claude. His health is much better and he is again playing with his chamber music ensemble. He is very happy about this. In fact, his ensemble will be performing in a few cities, including San Francisco, Boise, and—you'll never *believe this—St. George, which is very close to you! He will be there on March 15, and would very much like to visit with you. I have told him that, unfortunately, this is against the rules and not possible. But he wanted you to know about his plans and that he will be thinking of you when he performs nearby.*

I hope you continue to progress at your school. Please mind your teachers and listen to your therapists. Spring is coming soon. And that means fireflies aren't long after.

Love,
Dad

"It's from Jed," I told the girls at our weekly meeting. I was beaming. "I can't believe it. I haven't been able to get a letter out to him because there's been so much snow and all the field trips have been canceled. I thought for sure he'd given up on me. But it was like he knew how low I was feeling, and just when I thought I couldn't take it anymore, he sends me this."

"Brit. Stop," V said. "Breathe."

I stopped. I breathed. V held her hand out. "May I?"

"Go ahead. Read it aloud."

When she was finished, V looked at me and said, "I suppose you'll be wanting to claim your Christmas present now."

"Yes please."

"Will someone explain what's going on? I don't get it," Martha said.

"Yeah. I'm lost," said Cassie.

"Uncle Claude—that's Clod, my band. They're going on tour. They're coming to St. George, and Jed wants me to sneak out and meet him. At least I think that's what it says."

"That was my interpretation, darling," Bebe concurred.

"V, how are we gonna do this?" I asked.

We all turned to V, expecting her to stop and ponder, but she immediately launched into a plan: "Okay, here's the deal. There's supposed to be a Level Five and Six field trip sometime next week, so barring another blizzard, Cassie or I will make sure that one of us gets a spot. It's pretty easy to sneak away, and one of us will call my moles to see if they can pick you up. You'll use the pass key to unlock the door. I'll leave it in the fake plant next to Clayton's office. And listen up, because this is the fun part. At night most of the doors are alarmed, but here's the trick: If a door's left open, its alarm system isn't activated. So on the day of the concert, one of us is going to have to fake sick, get sent to the infirmary, and jam a piece of paper in the doorjamb on the way back. Brit, you just go to bed as usual.

"Now the goon goes to get his coffee at ten thirty, and then he takes a piss. I hear him walk by every night. That's your window, Brit. You'll sneak out to the infirmary, climb the big cottonwood tree, and hop the fence. It's not easy, but it can be done. Your ride will be waiting for you. You'll be back by morning roll call, and you'll get in the same way you got out."

V stopped. We all stared at her, our mouths hanging open. "*What.* I've had a lot of time to consider this."

"What are you still doing here, Moses? You obviously could've pulled an exodus ages ago." Cassie was stunned.

"I could've, but where would I go?"

"What about the cameras?" I asked.

V shrugged. "Look, this is risky. You'll for sure be

seen by the cameras, but the question is, will anyone see what the camera catches? No one watches the closed-circuit TV, and they just recycle the tapes over and over. You know how cheap and lazy this place is."

"It seems really risky, Brit," Martha warned.

"I don't care. I'd walk through fire to see Jed. What do I do about Helga, the nurse?"

"She doesn't sleep here."

"What about Tiffany?" Martha asked.

"Has Tiffany ever noticed you three missing for our meetings?"

"No."

"We always make sure she's sleeping before we leave," Bebe said. "She snores like a freight train." "And this will be less risky because only one of you is leaving. Brit, bunch some pillows under the covers so it looks like you're in bed."

"That solves the logistics. But there's another problem."

"Birth control?" Bebe asked. "You can get condoms in town, or maybe not. It's really Mormon around here."

"Bebe! I'm not having sex with Jed. That's not what I'm talking about. I was just wondering what to wear. All I have is this lame uniform."

The girls fell silent for a second. "Oh, that *is* a conundrum," Bebe said. "We can fix up your hair and do your makeup with my stash of beauty products. But fashion-wise? You might be stuck."

"I'm sorry, but I haven't seen Jed and the rest of them for six months and I'm going to be mortified if I have to show up in chinos and a polo shirt."

"I'd be mortified too, darling."

"What about the clothes we were wearing when we got here? Does anyone know where they are?" I asked. I'd had on a vintage skirt and a Clash T-shirt. It wasn't exactly sexy, but it was better than nothing.

"I was wearin' my pj's. They nabbed me at night," Cassie said.

"Me too," Bebe said. "Though lingerie might not be too bad."

"I don't think she's after the harlot look, Bebe," Cassie said.

"It doesn't matter," V interrupted. "They keep all that stuff, along with everything else they confiscate, in a locked closet in Sheriff's office. Let's not blow the whole plan by trying to break in."

"What about your secret agents in town?"

"They're nice and helpful, but of the sweats and sneakers variety," V said. "And much bigger than you."

"You could make something," Martha piped up.

"Out of what?" I asked.

"Maybe we could take a pair of shorts and pull out the seams and stitch them into a cute A-line skirt. That wouldn't be so bad. And you could take the polo shirt and rip off the sleeves and collar and turn it inside out, so it looks kind of frayed and rough. And you could wear knee socks and your Converse shoes. That would be kinda punk, right?"

"Slutty schoolgirl? Martha darling, you're a genius," Bebe said.

"Can you do any of that stuff?" I asked.

"Sure," Martha said sweetly, "but I'll need a needle and thread and something to pull the seams out with."

"I can smuggle that stuff from Home Ec," Cassie said.

"They have Home Ec here?" Bebe asked. "How did I not know that?"

"I think it's just for the, well, you know."

"Ahh, the Ellens . . ."

"Ellens?" Martha asked.

"As in DeGeneres," Bebe explained.

"Yeah, it's part of their plan to domesticate me. If I told 'em I wanted to sew, I could probably lay my hands on a needle and thread. I mean how much damage can you do with one little pin?"

Martha looked like she was about to burst with excitement. "Brit, I promise I'll do a good job. I used to make all my costumes."

"Costumes?" the four of us asked in unison.

"From when I was a Junior Miss."

"You were a beauty queen?" Cassie asked.

"Yeah. I was Miss Junior Columbus, Ohio, when I was twelve."

We all stared at her, completely astonished. *Martha?* A beauty queen? It wasn't that she wasn't pretty. She was. She had big green eyes and pretty pink skin. But Martha was a big girl, and she carried herself like she was trying to disappear. She just didn't have the aura of a Junior Miss.

"Martha darling. Don't take this the wrong way, but was it a plus-size beauty contest?" Leave it to Bebe. We'd all been thinking the same thing, but only she had the nerve to say it.

"It was a normal contest, Bebe, but I was skinny then," Martha said wistfully. "I only ballooned a few years ago. I guess my metabolism crashed," she said, looking down at her hands. "But I can still sew. Really, my costumes were gorgeous."

"Martha," V said. "You are a woman of mystery."

"I am?" she asked.

"You are," V replied. And with that Martha smiled a dazzling smile, and you could almost see the beauty queen within.

Chapter 15

"How awful is it? Are they mistreating you? With-holding food? We saw them do that to one inmate."

It was the night of March 15th and I was being smuggled to St. George with Beth and Ansley. V's plan had worked perfectly. It hadn't snowed again. Cassie had gone on a bowling field trip and slipped away to call our moles. Bebe had faked a case of food poison-ing and jammed the infirmary door open, and Martha had worked magic transforming the Red Rock uni-form into an almost-hip outfit. At twenty minutes after lights-out, I snuck out of my room, down the hall, out the door, up the tree, and over the fence, not even skin-ning my knee. When I saw Beth's pickup truck waiting for me, I couldn't believe how easy it was.

Beth and Ansley were chatty and dying to know about Red Rock. Normally I'd have welcomed the chance to spread the word about the fraudulent therapy going down there, but I was too busy trying to avoid puking. My stomach was in knots. I'd spent the previous three weeks worrying about V's master plan, imagining all the worst-case scenarios, having horrid nightmares about Sheriff grabbing my arm as I went out the door or Clayton and my dad waiting for me on the other side of the fence. In fact, I'd been so busy obsessing about my prison break that I hadn't really given much thought to *why* I was breaking out: to see Clod, to see Jed.

But now I was about to be reunited with my band—except they weren't my band anymore. I was going to be a spectator this time. Which was going to be weird. And speaking of weird—Jed. His letters, his affection, his distant support—he'd been like my firefly the last six months, something to light up the dreariness of Red Rock. I thought about him all the time, way more than I would've if I had my normal, full life. Way more, I was sure, than he'd been thinking about me. "Firefly" was probably just his way of being nice and encouraging. Riding toward town, I tried to let go of my well-nursed fantasies and started steeling myself for a major disappointment. It would be good to see Jed, and Denise and Erik anyhow, I told myself.

If I could find them. All I knew was that Clod was playing in St. George. I had no idea where or what time. It would be eleven o'clock at the earliest by the time I got there, and they might be long gone.

"Oh, no problem. St. George is dinky. There are only a couple of places where a band could play. We'll swing by Java Jive and Cafenomica," Ansley said.

"I'm sure they'll be playing at one of those," Beth added.

"We don't get many new bands in town," Ansley said. "Utah isn't exactly known for its music scene."

"Yeah, this is a real treat. We're going to go to the show too, if you don't mind," Beth said.

"No, that's great. I can't tell you how much I appreciate your help."

"It's nothing. We're glad to do it. We wish we could do more for you girls," Ansley said, "like getting that dump shut down."

We arrived in town, a cute place full of motels and galleries selling Indian art. At a stoplight, we saw a bunch of skater kids loitering near the corner. Ansley rolled down her window and asked if they knew where a band called Clod was playing, and we got the answer we were hoping for: Cafenomica.

I saw Denise first. She was onstage tinkering with the bass amp. "Brit, Oh my God!" she screamed as she ran toward me, tackling me in the world's hugest hug. "It's Brit. She made it. She made it!" she shouted to the crowd. "C'mon, the guys are out back. They're gonna shit a brick when they see you. And your timing is perfect. We're on at eleven thirty."

We went out to the parking lot, and there was the Vanagon, just like always. Erik was leaning against it, smoking a cigarette and talking to some girls. He waved wildly when he saw me, and then motioned for me to wait a second. He ran to the back of the van and pulled out a grease-stained paper bag. "Dude, you made it. I knew you would," he said, handing me the bag.

I sniffed it. "You got me a burrito?" I asked.

"Yah. Naturally. It's tradition. Except we already ate ours."

"Erik had the munchies," Denise said.

"I'll bet you did," I said, hugging him tightly. "Thanks."

"You're not gonna cry over a burrito, are you? I can't deal when chicks cry," Erik said.

I wiped my eyes. "No, I'm not gonna cry. I'm just happy to see you guys, that's all."

"We're happy to see you too, Brit." I heard his voice first. It sent a shiver up my spine. Then I felt his hand on my shoulder and my skin went hot where he touched it. I slowly turned around to face him, drinking in the sight of him. He was as beautiful as ever with his sleepy green eyes, his hair curling down around the nape of his neck. He leaned over to kiss my cheek but I turned my head and he kind of hit me on the side of the mouth. It was like a bolt of electricity went through me.

"Hi Jed," was all I could manage.

"Hi Brit." Jed smiled.

"Hi Jed," I said again.

Erik interrupted us. "Dudes, hate to cut the reunion short, but we gotta go play."

"Oh, of course. I'll just meet you guys after. I wanna get a good seat."

"Seat?" Jed looked at me like I must have been kidding. "You're playing too."

"I am?"

"Of course you are," Jed insisted. "You're a quarter Clod."

"But not anymore. You guys are totally doing awesome." I tried not to sound disappointed. "And besides, it's been six months. Who knows if I'll even remember how to play."

"You will," Jed said.

"But I don't have my guitar."

"Oh man, wait here," Erik said, and ran to the back of the van again. He pulled out my Gibson SG, my old friend.

"Where did you get this?" I wrapped my arms around my guitar as if it could hug me back.

"Girl, you're losing it," Denise said. "It was in Jed's basement, where you left it."

"Waiting for you," Jed said, looking straight into my eyes. I felt faint again.

"But I'm out of practice, and you must have new songs . . ."

"Can we stop it with the excuses already? Are you

not the Brit who barged her way into this band through sheer attitude even though you were just a kid and hardly knew how to play?" Denise asked.

I hoped I still was. "Yeah, I'm still that girl," I said tentatively.

"Well then, shut up already, and get tuned." Denise gave me her best tough chick look.

"Here's set list A," Jed said. "Golden oldies. All songs you know."

"What was set list B?" I asked.

"The one with newer stuff. We would have played that if you didn't show," Jed admitted.

"But wouldn't you rather . . . ?"

Jed cut me off. "We have plenty of other shows to play that stuff. Tonight, we're doing this set."

"Brit, will you stop it with the questions? Do you think we came to *Utah* because of its punk-rock pedigree?" Denise asked. "We came to play a show with you."

"You did?"

"Oh dude. She is gonna cry," Erik said. "Let's go."

● ● ●

Clod's first gig was in Eugene. I was a bundle of nerves before it started, even though it was just a backyard keg party near the university. When we set up, I was shaking so much I thought I wouldn't be able to strum or sing or remember the lyrics to our songs. But then we switched on the amps, and Jed sent a wave of feedback out. The crowd quieted, Erik counted back on his drumsticks, and we started playing. All of a sudden, it wasn't like I was in front of a crowd, or even with the rest of the band. I was alone with the music and it all just came to me instinctively. We played for a half hour, but it went by like it was seconds. When we finished, I was in a daze. Then, after, I was completely giddy. I couldn't stop laughing all night. Erik was convinced I was stoned.

When Erik clipped his drumsticks for the start of "Dumbbell" at Cafenomica, I went into a similar trance. The last six months—no, *the last few years*—just washed away from me. I was Brit again. The girl who did what she wanted to. The girl who had a mom and dad who loved her. The girl who had a regular, if slightly eccentric, life. It was like the music healed me, giving me back myself, my confidence, reminding me that the last six months weren't my real life. Real life was something wonderful, and though it seemed far away to me at the time, it still existed. *I* still existed.

We finished the set and bounded backstage. The crowd was going berserk. "Boy, they're really digging us," Denise said.

"They probably don't get much music out here," Erik said. I wanted to tell him that that was what Ansley had said to me, but I couldn't get my mouth to work. The crowd was still clapping, pounding on the tables, chanting "more."

"I think we have to go back out there," Jed said.

"What should we play?" Denise asked.

"I dunno," Jed said. "That was our entire set."

"I know. You guys go out and play something without me. It's cool."

"No. No way," Jed said. "That chanting out there, it's for all of us. We'll just do a cover."

"Covers are a cop-out." Clod did covers at practices, for fun, but we never played them at live shows. It was a point of pride with us. "I have an idea," I said. "Okay guys, listen. It's a straight G, D, A minor. Ballady. If I start, can you just fall in? It's pretty basic."

"G, D, A minor. I can handle that," Jed said. "You

got it?" he nodded to Denise.

"And slowish, Erik. I know you like speed but this one's quiet. Use your brushes."

"Got it. Mellow."

I went out on the stage and picked up my guitar. "This song is for my Sisters. And for my band, too. It's called 'I Got Your Back.' Ready, guys?" And then I started strumming, and as always Jed picked up the riff, followed by Denise and Erik, and it was like we all knew the song, like we'd always played it. After I finished, the audience was on its feet, stamping and screaming. We all waved and ran offstage.

"Is it just me, or was that the greatest show?" Denise gushed.

"It wasn't just you," Jed said quietly. "This was special."

Afterward, we loaded up and, just like old times, went to Denny's and gorged ourselves. I ordered blueberry pancakes, a burger and fries, a shake, and of course endless cups of coffee. Maybe it was the show or my nerves, or maybe Denny's food tasted unbelievably delicious after six months of Red Rock freeze-dried crap. When the waitress brought out my multiple entrees, everyone laughed, but then they seemed concerned.

"They starving you in there?" Denise said.

"Hmm, nrot quwrite," I said, mouth full.

"This girl always could pack away her body weight in food," Erik said. "But chill with the coffee or you won't sleep."

"I don't care. We're not allowed coffee in that place. Can you imagine six months without a cup of coffee?"

"Whoa, they *are* starving you in there. Isn't there some human-rights law about denying coffee?" Like most people from Portland, Denise took her caffeine addiction very seriously.

"I wish," I said.

"So this Denny's swill must taste like champagne," Jed said.

"The Dom Perignon of java," I admitted.

"Life without good coffee. Dude, it makes you appreciate what you've got," Erik said.

"Amen to that," Jed said, looking at me kind of funny.

As we ate, they caught me up on all the latest news on the Clod-front. After the Indian Summer Festival that I missed, they'd been booked all over Oregon and

Washington, in clubs, even in some bigger venues opening for other bands. A couple of indie labels were talking about making a single, or maybe even a whole CD. They kept reassuring me that when I got back, my place was still there, and they weren't looking for a replacement. "We make a decent trio," Denise said. "But we're better as a foursome."

"Hear, hear," Erik said, holding up his cup.

Around two, Denise and Erik started yawning. Denise pointed to her watch. "We should probably get some shut-eye," she said.

"Are you driving out tonight?" I asked. We often napped in the back of the van before driving on after a show.

"Nah. Next stop is Spokane, which is miles from here. But we don't have to be there until the day after tomorrow, so we're crashing at a Motel 6."

"Wow, motels. You guys are big-time now."

"We make enough at the door now to at least cover the tour. And to pay for your enormous meal," Erik said as he swooped up the bill.

We made our way back to the van, Erik making a big show of letting me ride shotgun. I was still feeling giddy and way wired on the coffee, but as we drove through town, it hit me that the night was ending. I wasn't going on to Spokane and the next fun place. I was going back *there*. It was like someone turned the lights out and I got instantly depressed. A weird mood descended on all of us, no one talking or joking like we'd been just a few minutes before. When I spotted the Motel 6 sign in the distance, I felt empty inside, a huge pit in my Denny's-bloated stomach.

"What about you?" Jed asked me as he pulled into the driveway.

"What about me?"

"When do you have to be back?"

"Roll call's at seven, but I should probably be back before it gets light. Around six, I guess."

"Do you feel like staying out? Maybe taking a drive? I don't want to get you busted—"

"No," I interrupted. "I mean, don't worry about me. I want to stay out."

"I'm glad. Me too," he said.

When we dropped off Denise and Erik at the motel, they gave me a giant group hug. I felt sad to see them go but also so excited to be alone with Jed—at least for a few hours.

"You hang in there, girl."

"Thanks, Denise. I'll be okay."

"I know you will."

"Here's a little something to get you through the rough times," Erik said, offering me a Baggie full of pot.

"No thanks, Erik."

"Really? It's the kind bud."

"Moron. She doesn't even smoke, and she's like in prison," Denise said. "Sorry, Brit."

"No, it's fine. Thanks, Erik. I appreciate the thought."

"Okay, we'll see you back in P-town," he said.

"Absolutely." I gave them one last hug good-bye, then I climbed back into the van with Jed. "So, where are you taking me?"

"I thought we'd drive into the mountains. Zion National Park is pretty close to here. I went there with my grandparents once. It's got these really unusual rock formations, all named after Mormon prophets. It's intense. I don't know how much we can see at night, but we've almost got a full moon." He pointed out the window to where the moon was shining bright and white.

"It sounds great. I haven't seen much of the area."

"Don't you get out, to walk around or anything?

"Not really. They have these hikes when the weather is warmer, but they're more like marches. It's not about enjoying the scenery."

"It sounds awful, this place you're in. I looked it up on the Internet. Really scary stuff."

"You don't know the half of it."

"Do you want to tell me about it?"

"You know what? I'd rather just forget that place for tonight."

Jed smiled, but he looked sad. "What place?" he asked.

We drove along a winding road uphill. The moon was reflecting off the giant, sheer red cliffs jutting straight out of the canyons. I stared out the window in between sneaking glances at Jed—mainly at the side of his neck. I had such an urge to lick it, imagining the taste, salty with dried sweat. We wound through the mountains, Jed playing me songs that had been released within the last six months, music that I'd missed. After about a half hour, we pulled into a town called Springdale, and Jed parked the van. "I think this is the end of the road. The park starts now. We can just walk from here. If you want."

"I'd like that."

"Are you cold?"

I was freezing. All I had on was the skirt Martha had stitched me and a sweatshirt I'd borrowed from Ansley. I nodded. Jed pawed through the back and pulled out his beat-up brown suede jacket, the one he wore everywhere, the one I used to sneak sniffs of when he wasn't looking. "Here, you wear this. And I'll grab a blanket in case we need reinforcements."

We walked into the park and Jed tried to catch me up on life in Portland. He made me laugh with gossip about who was dating whom, which band had broken up, who had gotten a record deal. I had forgotten how easy it was to talk to him, and all my nerves from earlier in the evening vanished. We walked for a half hour, until we found ourselves in a grassy clearing next to a small river.

"Want to stop awhile?"

I wanted to stop for more than a while. I wanted to freeze-frame the night, leave it so it would go on forever, even though I had to be back in a few hours. But I just said yes. Jed spread out the blanket, and we lay down. The sky was amazing, full of millions of stars and so crisp you could see the Milky Way. "I forgot how clear it was out here," Jed said. I was lying right next to him, so close I could see the faint veins in his earlobes. I reached over and squeezed his wrist.

"Thank you, Jed."

"For what?"

"For everything. For the letters, for dragging the band to Utah. For this," I said, gesturing to the sky.

He took my hand and stroked my palm. "I didn't do it for you," he said in a quiet voice. "Not entirely." Then he took both my hands in his grasp and kissed me on the inside of each wrist, moving his way up with feathery kisses to my elbows, my shoulders, my neck. By the time he reached my lips, my whole body was humming with anticipation, and the kiss itself, it was like melting chocolate. We stayed there for a while, kissing and touching. And then Jed started to laugh.

"God, I've been wanting to do that for too long."

"You have? Then why didn't you, you moron?" I said, smacking him on the chest before burying my face into his neck and at long last licking it like my own personal lollipop. He kissed me again, all over my face, then pulled away and brushed the hair out of my eyes.

"At first I just thought you were too young. Then it was because I didn't want to mess things up with the band. And then you were going through all that personal crap and I didn't want to add another complication to your life."

"You're not a complication. You're the opposite of a complication. You and the band were the two good, effortless things in my life."

"And you, Brit, are a rock star. Don't let anyone make you feel like any less."

"I won't."

"Promise me."

"I will if you promise to stop talking now."

Jed grinned as he reached for me again.

* * *

That night, after we fell asleep under the blanket, after I woke up with my head on Jed's chest, I took a sense-memory picture. It was something my mom had taught me to do, to record how a place sounded, looked, smelled, tasted, and felt. That way, if something was really special, you could take it with you, summon it at any time. I pulled up memories of my mom that way a lot, and I knew I'd be calling up this night again. As I was recording everything, listening to Jed's heart thump in my ear, I saw a shooting star flame across the sky, like the world's biggest firefly.

Chapter 16

Later that morning, back in the dorm, I could still taste Jed on me, could smell him, feel the spot on my chin that had been rubbed raw by his stubble. It already felt like a dream, the whole night—Jed driving me back, telling me I didn't have to go, that I could just stay with him, go back to Portland. I wanted to say yes, but I knew that wasn't the answer. I had to figure out how to get out of Red Rock free and clear. I had to get my life back. Jed said he understood and promised that he and Clod would be waiting for me when I got home. Then I snuck back into the room, where Bebe was laying awake in her bed. She flashed me a thumbs-up sign with a questioning look and I flashed her a thumbs-up back, along with the world's goofiest grin. She silently cheered and motioned for me to get into bed. I lay there, watching the sun come up through the shades, savoring the night.

At 6:30 A.M., the lights went on, and Sheriff's voice boomed over the speaker, "Rise and shine, girlies." I didn't want to erase Jed's scent by showering, so I just got dressed. At seven, I shuffled out to roll call. I had to clench my mouth shut to keep from smiling. Normally roll call was split by Levels—Three and Four in one group, and Five and Six in another—but this morning we were all ordered outside to the quarry. When I got out there, V sidled up next to me. "Something's up, something's happened," she hissed. "Whatever you do, don't say a thing. I mean it, Brit. Not a word." And then she disappeared to line up with all the Level Sixers.

The counselors came out and did the head count, same as they did every morning. When they were done, they went and conferred with one another and Sheriff. There hadn't been a school-wide roll call since I'd arrived, so this was a rare event. Everyone was buzzing, talking to one another about what was happening. V was giving me her sternest look. I had a bad feeling.

After some talk, Sheriff came back out. "I bet you girls think you're pretty smart," he began, scanning the crowd. "I bet you think you're so clever. Well, let me tell you, this ain't gonna end pretty. One of you girls decided to take a little night off, didn't you? We got a call this morning saying that someone had spotted a Red Rock uniform over in St. George. Nah, I thought. My girls are smarter than that. They know better. But just to be sure, we got out our surveillance tapes, and you know what we found? We found that someone here had broken the trust. We got it on tape."

Shit, shit, shit, shit, I thought to myself. I'm so screwed. But even as I knew I was about to get nailed, sent down the river to Level One or worse, part of me didn't care. I wouldn't have traded last night for the world.

"We got ourselves a bit of a problem," Sheriff said. "It's dark. And we don't have a good shot of who it was, but we've got some ideas. And trust me, we're going to find out just who our runaway is. So before we get into this further, I'm giving the guilty party this one opportunity to step forward."

V was practically burning holes through me with her eyes, her brows in full-arch mode. I kept my mouth shut.

"I can't say I'm surprised. A liar, a cheat, and a rat, that's who the guilty girl is. And rats don't come out easy, but there's ways to smoke 'em out. You girls are gonna help, too. Starting now. If anyone knows who our runaway is and wants to tell us about it, step forward. I can promise you, you'll be rewarded."

Tiffany! She would fink me out in a second. She'd been snoring when I left, but who knew if she'd woken up to pee and saw that I was missing. I stared at her and saw that Bebe was looking her way too. But Tiffany was watching Sheriff with rapt attention. She was too dumb to fake dumb. She didn't know.

"Again, I can't say I'm surprised, girlies. Disappointed, but not surprised. So how about we add a little incentive to the pot, something to motivate you girls into helping us find our guilty party? As of right now, you are all dropped down a level."

A yell erupted from the crowd. "No way." "That's not fair!" "It's not our fault." Everyone protested.

"Quiet!" yelled Sheriff. "You're right, it's not fair.

But we're a family here and we take responsibility for each other's actions. One of you girls broke the rules. So this is the way it's gonna be until we figure out who ran out last night. Now here's where you girls can help yourselves. I know that some of you must know what happened. Whoever did this didn't act alone, is my hunch. So here's our little game. You have a week, and in that week I want to find out who ran out last night. If any one of you names the culprit in a week, you'll all be restored to your current levels. If you don't, you'll drop down again. Is that understood?"

Another wail went up among the girls. Some were crying. I had to hand it to Sheriff. He was more clever than I'd pegged him to be. And his plan was successful. I knew that the Sisters would never give me up, but there was no way I was going to let everyone drop a level. I took a deep breath and started to work my way through the crowd.

"That won't be necessary, Mr. Austin," V said, striding forward, just as Bebe yanked me back by my collar. "I did it. I'm the one who went to St. George."

Just like that, everyone was silent, and then in unison, everyone gasped.

"Larson, why am I not surprised?" Sheriff said. "I will meet you in my office, girlie. The rest of you are restored to your levels, but let this be a warning: if any one of you runs out again, I will knock all of you down a peg, immediately. So you might want to keep a close watch on each other, to prevent this kind of breach from happening again. Now get to breakfast."

The crowd shuffled away, atwitter with all the drama. As our unit walked by, Sheriff called out "Hemphill, Howarth, Wallace, Jones, you come here." Bebe, Martha, Cassie, and I slunk over. "Don't think I haven't noticed the little club you girlies have formed for yourselves. Don't think for a second I think any of you is innocent in this monkey business. Just so you know, I'm gonna be watching you very closely, waiting for you to slip up, and when you do, I'm gonna be there to kick your butts. Now get out of my sight," he said, wiping the saliva from his lips.

Silently, we walked toward the cafeteria. All around us, the other girls were giddy with gossip. "Can you believe it? God, that was so stupid," one Level Three girl said.

"I know. Like, she's Level Six. She's about to get out. Why would she blow it like that?"

I was wondering the very same thing.

As I walked down the hall, I saw her there, standing outside Sheriff's office, looking small, with a goon guard on either side of her. She was staring at me, trying to impart one of her silent cryptic messages. I knew she wanted me to look back at her, to receive the message. I knew that I should. I should be grateful. She saved my ass, took my fall. But I couldn't look at her and I wasn't grateful. I was furious.

Chapter 17

"Are you going to leave your bed like that?" Missy asked me.

"Am I going to leave my bed like what?"

"All messy. Your sheets aren't even tucked in."

"You're not serious."

"I most certainly am. Pride in your home space is a sign of self-respect."

"You caught me. I have no respect for myself."

"You're being sarcastic, right? It's *so* not funny."

"A sense of humor is a sign of self-deprecation," I said and turned away, leaving my rumply bed rumpled.

Of the various maladies that had befallen the

Sisters in Sanity, Missy was among the worst. Two days after my breakout, the day after V was stripped of her Level Six status, Sheriff began to make good on his threat. At roll call that next day, one of the counselors informed me that as of that night, I would no longer be rooming with Bebe and Martha. After dinner, I was marched to a room in the other wing to find my stuff had already been moved, and I had a new roommate. Missy was the queen of the Stockholm-syndrome girls and one of Red Rock's greatest success stories. After her parents enrolled her for ditching school to smoke pot a couple of times, she'd had a full-on turnaround and now she was a born-again good girl who loved to work her program and who gushed about being in AA like it was a sorority. When prospective parents wanted to know more about Red Rock, Sheriff would have Missy call them up and spew crap about how the school had saved her life. She was on the promotional video. Her picture was in the brochures.

As I unpacked, Missy watched me through squinted eyes, like she was trying to x-ray my stuff. When I went to the bathroom to brush my teeth, she followed me and kept staring as I flossed.

"Do you mind?" I asked.

"Yes. I do. I mind that you've been here six months and you've made no progress. I mind that you have an attitude. And I mind that you've wasted everyone's time. But now, you're mine to mind."

I just stared at her. She couldn't be serious.

The rest of the Sisters were in similar sinking boats. Bebe had been moved into a room with a Sixer named Hilary, another brochure girl who was pals with Missy and followed Bebe around just as doggedly as Missy did me. Cassie had also been moved, which made no sense because V was moved *out* of Cassie's room. It was a tough call, however, to say who had it the worst: V or Martha. Martha still roomed with Tiffany, but the newly promoted Tiffany was on a crazy Level Six power trip. And V? Well, usually when you got sent back to Level One for some offense, you stayed in isolation for a few days at most before starting the long climb back up the level ladder, but after three weeks, V was still in her little room, shoeless and wearing her frayed pj's all day. The powers that be were really pissed off, and they were taking it out on V for what I'd done. Maybe I should've felt sorry for her or relieved or grateful, but when I thought about V, I still felt mad.

· · ·

"I can't say that I didn't warn you about Virginia Larson," Clayton said to me in a session after the breakout. She had that self-satisfied look on her face, the one that made me want to throw something at her.

"You did warn me," I said, hoping that would stop the conversation in its tracks. No such luck.

"I told you she was a bad influence, that your mere association with her would have negative repercussions for you. It's a fact of life that sometimes the actions of others rub off on us, and we have to take responsibility. And now you're forced to accept responsibility for V's *ir*responsibility. Isn't that ironic, Brit?"

It was actually more ironic than she knew, and though this was one of the few times I agreed with Clayton, I wasn't about to say so. I halfway suspected that she knew the truth and was hinting at it to bait me. Sheriff, on the other hand, took the more blatant tack. Every time I saw him, he pointed to his eyes with two cocked fingers and then pointed them back at me. "I'm watching you, Hemphill. Waiting for a slip-up."

Whatever. With the constant surveillance, things were pretty depressing around Red Rock. The one bright spot was Jed. Less than a week after the show, I got a letter from him.

Dear Brit:

How are you? I hope you are well and are doing fine in school, not having any trouble or anything like that. I'm sure I would've heard about it. You're a smart girl and I trust you are progressing fine.

Not much to report here since my last letter. It's springtime and we've had some spectacular days. Of course, it's still freezing, but that doesn't stop all the students in town from running around in shorts and sandals. I stay warm in my favorite suede jacket. It has such a nice smell to it.

Uncle Claude has returned from his tour and I thought you'd like to know that he said he enjoyed Utah very much. Apparently, the concert was well received and Claude had some extra time to visit the surrounding national parks. A most memorable visit, he said. He told me to tell you that Zion was the most beautiful place he'd ever been and when you graduate from your school, he'd like to go there with you.

I'm fine. In good health, though I had a little rash on my neck. My colleagues teased me that it looked like a hickey. Imagine that.

It's a very busy time at work right now, lots of reports to write up, so you'll forgive me if this letter is short. If I wrote everything in my heart, this might go on for days.

So, suffice it to say, I miss you.
Dad

Swoon. I was dying to get the Sisters together, to tell them about everything that had happened, but there was just no way. Martha and I were forced to sit at opposite ends of the room in class, so no more note passing, and I couldn't even get next to Bebe in group without Missy sneaking up or Hilary bounding between us.

A few weeks after the breakout and still no contact with the Sisters. I was starting to go batty. In order to keep myself from falling off the cliff into true depression, I called up my night with Jed constantly, reliving every moment. It kept me sane. And then when I thought things couldn't get any bleaker, Clayton pulled one of her infamous head games.

"I'm going to have some news about your mother," she told me at the end of a session. "So prepare yourself."

Aside from Clayton's occasional attempts to get me to go deeper about Mom, we hadn't talked much about her. In fact, it had been years since anyone had seriously discussed my mother with me. Dad hadn't. Stepmonster certainly didn't. Even Grandma had stopped bringing her up much. It was as though she had died, even though we knew she was out there. In the beginning, when she first went away, I'd jump every time the phone rang, but after a few months, I stopped hoping she'd call.

"What news?"

"I'm not at liberty to discuss that with you yet."

"How can you not be at liberty to discuss it? She's my mom!"

"I'm on vacation next week, so we'll talk about it when I get back."

"Why the hell would you bring it up if you can't tell me about it? Do you like to torture me?"

Clayton smiled. "No, I don't like to torture you. I'm giving you this heads-up because I need you to be prepared to open up, to work your issues."

Two weeks? I suppose I could've asked Dad what happened to Mom, but if he knew something was up, why hadn't *he* told me anything? His letters had been focused on Billy's latest tricks and my recent report card. And they said *I* was in denial! That was *it*. I needed to talk to the girls. In group that afternoon, I passed Bebe a note.

> *BB:*
> *Must meet. So much going on w/*
> *Clayton, Jed—and Mom. Am going*
> *crazy w/ silent treatment. Am going*
> *crazy, period. Help.*
> *—Cinders*

Cinders:
Am desperate for powwow with my
darlings. Can you get away tonight?
   —BB

BB:
YES!!! I'll get the key.
   —Cinders

Cinders:
Parfait. You alert Martha. I'll tell
Cass. V's <u>still</u> in iso. ☹
   —BB

· · ·

"I hate her," I wailed to the girls. "She's so cruel. Can you imagine?" I'd just finished telling them about my latest conversation with Clayton.

"God, she's the worst. She's like a lion, sniffing around for weakness so she can pounce," Bebe said. "She loves to natter on about how I have sex because I think I'm unlovable, and contrary to trying to show me the folly of my thinking, it's like she agrees! Stupid cow is just jealous. I'm sure she hasn't been laid since before any of us was born."

"You think *that's* bad? She tells me that I'm an embarrassment to my parents!" Martha cried. "She says that I got fat to get back at my mom. Everything I do is to punish my parents, according to her."

"That's what she said about me," Cassie said quietly. "That I was so angry with my folks I had to go and become this abomination."

Bebe shuddered. "Let's not talk about that evil wench, darlings. What else is happening? Are you all enjoying your new bodyguards? How's our little Tiffany?"

"Awful," Martha said. "It's like she's taking all of her wrath out on me. What have I ever done to her? She even watches me eat now, and those bulimics know every trick in the book, so I can't hide food in my socks anymore."

"God, how horrific, darling. I empathize. My guard Hilary is of the kill-'em-with-kindness school, and I'm her new pet. She's like this sparkly Mormon girl. Honestly, she's got to be a plant, because there's no way that girl could've ever done anything remotely delinquent enough to land her at Red Rock. She's a virgin, for Chrissakes. She even took one of those chastity pledges, and she's after me to reclaim my virginity. Seriously, please tell her I can't get it back."

"I'm a virgin," Martha declared.

"I reckon I am too, technically," Cassie said.

"Never mind that, girls. My point is," Bebe continued, "that she's like a Mousketeer, and my most evil barbs don't penetrate her do-goodery armor. God, I think I've met my match."

"I doubt that," I said.

"Everything is so rotten right now," Martha said. "V's gone. We have to sneak around. Sheriff has been forcing me to go on death marches, and now I have to go on weekly overnight expeditions. Tell me something good, Brit. Tell me about Jed."

So I did. I told the girls about my amazing night out, and the letter Jed just sent me.

"God, it's so romantic. You have a boyfriend," Martha said.

"Do I?"

"Secret dates, sneakin' love letters. Y'all have a Romeo-and-Juliet scenario happenin'," Cassie said.

"I don't know if he's my boyfriend, but he's the

thing that keeps me from going crazy in here. Besides you guys, of course."

"I know, darling. Me too. And if it's bad for us, can you imagine how poor V is faring? Three weeks in isolation."

"Cruel and unusual punishment," Cassie said.

"You must be so grateful," Martha said. "She did all this for you, so you could be with Jed."

I paused for a second. "I am."

Everyone looked at me expectantly, like they wanted more.

"I sense a 'but,'" Bebe said.

"What do you mean?"

"You seem a little off about this."

"No I'm not."

"Don't BS a BS-er, Brit," Bebe said.

"I'm not off. It's just what she did was enormous and all, but don't you think it's a little weird that she did it?"

"Do I think it's weird that she took the fall for you?" Bebe asked.

"Yeah, that she'd blow it for herself when she was so close to graduating. It's not the first time she's done something like this, and I just thought it was a little, you know, odd."

"What's odd is that you seem so ungrateful that she took a bullet for you," Bebe said with ice in her voice.

"I'm not ungrateful. It just made me feel, I don't know how to explain it, but . . ."

"She was watching your back, Brit," Martha said.

"You know, to fend off the monsters' attack. Those're your words, aren't they?" Cassie looked at me like I'd completely disappointed her.

I took a deep breath. "Look, you guys, I'm not trying to diss V, and I feel horrible for what's happened to her, responsible even. I should be the one locked up in iso, not her."

"V turns eighteen in a few months, so she probably knew that she'd get outa here sooner than you would if you got dumped down to Level One," Cassie said. "She's a smart girl, that one. She's got her reasons."

"Maybe," I said.

"Remind me never to do you a favor," Bebe said. "No good deed goes unpunished."

"That's not fair, Bebe. And this isn't about you, so stop being such a bitch."

"I'm the bitch? Please. And this *is* about me. V is my friend."

"Oh, and I'm not, is that it?"

"Please stop fighting," Martha pleaded. "You sound like my parents."

"Yeah, you two tomcats, cut it out," Cassie said.

Bebe and I just glared at each other, arms crossed around our chests while Martha and Cassie talked. Then it was three in the morning and I went back to my room with a new pit in my stomach about V and Bebe, lodged next to the one about Mom.

Chapter 18

Those were about the longest two weeks of my life. No news about Mom. No more Sisters meetings. V finally came off Level One, but every time I saw her, she was shadowed by two Level Six girls or a counselor. Bebe wasn't looking at me, let alone talking to me. Martha was always MIA—Red Rock had her on a strict schedule of death marches. And Cassie was glued to her new roommate, Laurel. No letters from Jed. No distractions. Nothing to think about but Mom.

When Clayton came back, looking neither tan nor rested nor bearing any visible signs of a fun vacation, I was polite. I asked her about her trip. Then I asked her about Mom.

Clayton leaned back in her chair and twirled the pen in her hand. She adjusted the air-conditioning knob and straightened the notebooks on her table. Then she opened my file and pulled out a letter. From the looping cursive, I knew it was from Grandma. From the tape on the back of the envelope, I knew it had been opened. I looked at the postmark: Monterey, California, dated almost four weeks ago.

"You've had this letter a month?"

"Something like that."

"So why did you make me wait?"

"I didn't think you were ready."

"That's not what you said. You said you weren't at liberty."

"Fine. I wasn't at liberty. I hadn't given myself the liberty to give you this letter. And now I have." Clayton glared at me, waiting for me to open the letter so she could pick over every last piece of it. I slipped the envelope into my back pocket. Clayton looked surprised.

"You were so anxious last session. I thought you'd want to read it right away."

"I don't want to waste our session. And whatever's in the letter will still be in it later," I said with a fake smile. The enveloped burned a hole in my pocket for the rest of the hour. As soon as it was up, I ran to the bathroom, where I could read it in peace.

My Dear Brittie:

How are you? I hope you are okay. I worry about you endlessly. Your father tells me you are in a special school, that you've been in some kind of trouble, but I just can't believe it. Not my girl. You've always had such a good head on your shoulders, so I know that if there is anything wrong, you'll work to fix it.

Are you warm enough out there in Utah? Are you eating enough? Can I send you some oatmeal bars? I would like to make a visit. I might even fly to see you. I'm getting used to airplanes now. I've actually flown quite a bit of late. I've been taking trips up to Spokane . . . to see your mother.

I probably should have told you about all this sooner, but I didn't want to get your hopes up, or down, depending.

About a year ago, I stopped hearing from Laura altogether. After spending months lying awake at night, imagining all the awful scenarios that could've befallen her, I hired a private investigator to track her down. Well, the first man I hired was a charlatan; he took a lot of money and did nothing. But after Christmas, I hired someone else. This gentleman, a former police detective from Los Angeles, found your mother in no time. She was living in a homeless shelter in Spokane, Washington.

As soon as the detective found her, I flew up to see her. I was hoping that she might come live with me, or even check into a good private hospital I found in Santa Barbara. But mostly, I just wanted to hold her, to make sure she was all right.

From what I can gather, your mother has been living in this shelter, which is more like a group home, for a few months. She is physically in good health. Mentally, I wish I had better news. One of the reasons I didn't tell you about my visit right away was that I didn't know how to break it to you. Your mother is very agitated still. She recognizes me one day and then doesn't respond the next. I showed her a picture of you and she froze up, refused to talk. I can't imagine what it's like to live inside her head, and you mustn't take anything she does personally. Your mother is mentally ill, but I know that deep down she loves you as she always has.

On the positive side, she has a group of what I suppose you could call friends and seems to have a little bit of a safety net. There are social workers who work at the shelter, so there's always someone keeping an eye out for her. On my first trip, I tried to persuade her to come back to California with me, to check into a hospital, but she refused. I flew back home all set to forcibly transfer her and then I thought better of it. She has a modicum of stability in her life right now. She's being looked

*after, to some degree, which is better than
nothing. She still refuses any kind of treatment, still thinks the doctors are all out to
get her, but my feeling is that maybe over
time, if I stay close to her, I can change her
mind.*

*Which brings me to my current plan. I
am going up to Spokane for the summer,
to be closer to Laura, to see if I can't gain
her trust, find a way to help her. There are
so many new medications she could bene-
fit from. I can't give up hope, and neither
should you. Laura probably won't ever be
the woman we once knew, and it may take
years to even get back some semblance of
the woman she was. But we've got to try,
right?*

*Oh, Brittie. This is all so hard, and I
know how difficult it must be for you. I
know you've been through so very much.
As has your father. Now that I have
become your mother's legal guardian, I
understand the weight of that responsibility. Don't be mad at your father for what*

he has done to you. He does it out of love.
I understand that now.
I love you, darling. Stay well.
Grandma

"I hear your crazy mother was found wandering the streets in Canada," Missy chirped to me, her eyes bright with enthusiasm. It was the following day in CT and, what a coincidence, I was in the mush pot. Sheriff was leading things, as he always seemed to these days.

"Spokane's in Washington. Learn some geography, why don't you. And how'd you hear?"

"I was told."

"By Clayton?" So much for patient confidentiality.

"That's not important," Missy said, with this great, big sympathetic look on her face. "We're here to help you process. Tell us how you feel."

"She's right, Hemphill. Own up to your feelings," Sheriff said.

"You tell me what you know," I said, facing Missy.

"Your grandmother tracked your mother down, found her living like, like some crazy homeless person," she said.

"Mama's a wild child, just like you," Sheriff said.

"Neither of you know crap about my mom."

"I know she lived in denial about her illness until it was too late," Missy said.

"Shut up!"

"Whoa, girlies. Looks like someone touched a nerve there," Sheriff said.

"Unless you get with the program, you're gonna end up just like her," Missy said.

"Missy, there is so much in the world that you don't know, that to even begin explaining it all to you would take the rest of my life." My voice came out steady, even though my insides were burning. "And I'd rather end up like my crazy, messed-up mother than spend even a moment as a conniving, cowardly little conformist like you!"

Everyone cracked up when I said that, even Sheriff, who loved nothing more than a good catfight. Missy's face went white with rage and finally she shut up. But when she caught my eye, she mouthed "I'm gonna get you."

Chapter 19

I couldn't sleep that night. I had so many emotions roiling around, about Mom—and Dad, as usual—but also about Missy, V, and Bebe. So I lay in bed and thought about writing Jed a letter. I'd been writing him a lot of imaginary letters lately. I'd gotten another note from him with fireflies drawn all over it, but I hadn't been able to sneak anything out to him. Hence my telepathic missives.

In my mind, I could say everything I really felt, things I never would have been able to say to Jed's face or in real letters. I told him about how much our night meant to me and about the feeling I'd had when I played with the band. The music had cleansed me of so much unhappiness, and in my mind my love of music and my love for him were all mixed up. I told him about my fight with Bebe and my weird feelings toward V. And sometimes when it was really quiet and late and I couldn't sleep, I would confide in Jed about the things that scared me most: that I'd never get out of Red Rock and get to be with him like a normal girl, that I never was or would ever be a normal girl. Maybe I was going to end up crazy too. Not the carving-my-skin, barfing-up-my-lunch, ditching-class types that passed for crazy at Red Rock. But voices-in-my-head crazy. Crazy like my mother.

I was still talking to Jed when the sun peeked through the shades. A day on the quarry with no sleep was a brutal thing, and I knew I was in for a rough go of it when I stumbled to the shower. And that was before I saw V crouching in the corner of the stall.

"Don't scream," she whispered as I jumped.

"How'd you get in here?" I whispered.

"Very sneakily," she said.

"Aren't you still Level Two?"

"Yes. But Level Two girls need showers too." V pointed to the dressing area, where her escort was waiting.

"How'd you know I'd be here?"

"You always use the second stall, Brit. For a rebel girl you're a creature of habit."

"Are you okay? We've all been worried sick about you. You must be going crazy in iso."

"It's not fun, but I've endured worse."

"Couldn't you just tell Sheriff that you were ready to face your issues?"

"I'm afraid that doesn't work the fourth time around," she said, smiling ruefully. "I was hoping I'd see one of you guys, thought you might slip over to see me."

"Well, it's been rough. We've all been under surveillance."

"There are ways around that."

I shrugged. "You're the one who knows all the ways. What were we supposed to do?"

"That's up to you."

"What—you think I owe you a risky visit because of what you did?"

V looked genuinely surprised and then kind of hurt, which made me feel like a jerk. "You don't owe me anything, Brit. There's no outstanding debt between us." She seemed sincere, but I felt like it was all a lie. There was a huge debt between us, and now I would have to pay her back for something I'd never asked for in the first place. "Don't sweat it. Your Christmas present was just more costly than I expected, but I was happy to give it to you. Did you have a good night out with Jed?"

I smiled just thinking of it. "I did."

"So be happy. It was worth it."

"To me, not to you."

"That's for me to decide. Are you mad at me or something?"

"Or something," I lied. "I just feel guilty."

"Brit," she sighed with all her world-weariness. "Guilt is such a waste of an emotion. Don't spend your energy on it—or on me." And then she crawled under the stall to the empty shower next to mine and turned on the tap.

That afternoon on the quarry was one of my loneliest times at Red Rock. The heat had returned in full force, sending the counselors back to their Diet Cokes and magazines on the patio. It would have been possible to talk to the girls. But Martha wasn't there, probably on another of her hikes. And Cassie was working alongside her new roommate again.

Bebe was still giving me the cold shoulder. So I just piled bricks by myself, replaying my sad conversation with V in my mind. It was so hot out and I was perspiring so much that no one noticed my face was damp with tears.

• • •

It was three long weeks before Bebe decided to end her silent treatment and make peace with me. Sort of. She approached me on the quarry, ready to strike a deal.

"This is all getting so tiresome, Brit," she said. "I'm bored with it. Can we stop now?" No apology. No "I missed you." No "darling."

"You're the one who's pissed at me, Bebe," I said.

"Look, I just said this whole thing was tiresome. Can we not talk about it? Besides, I have something far more amusing to tell you."

"What?"

"Come with me." I followed her over to where Cassie was piling bricks with her new roommate. "Brit, this is Laurel. Laurel, this is Brit." We checked each other out. Laurel was tiny, a speck of a thing, even smaller than Bebe, with black hair cut into a bob and gorgeous hazel eyes. Lucky girl to have Cassie as her brick buddy.

"Laurel is Cassie's new roommate."

"I know. Hi."

"Hey."

"It appears our Cassie and her Laurel are special roommates."

"Huh?" I asked. Laurel was standing right there, so I wasn't sure what Bebe was doing. Cassie, for her part, was pawing at the ground with her foot and blushing crimson.

"You know how being assigned new roommates was a punishment? Well they really found a way to nail Cass."

I looked at Laurel, but her face was impassive. I didn't know why Bebe was dissing her like this.

"They roomed Cassie with a lesbian!" Bebe said, cracking up now.

"I prefer the term *queer*," Laurel said.

Bebe laughed so loudly that Cassie had to cover her mouth with her hand.

"But the idiots that run this place obviously don't know I'm queer," Laurel said.

"Ain't that rich?" Cassie said. "Her mom put her here because she ran away to San Francisco when she was fifteen. But the reason she ran away is because she was afraid to come out in a small town with less than two hundred kids at her high school. Just like me."

"I ran away because I was *advised* to," Laurel said. "You see, when I started to feel too trapped to breathe, I called the national gay-lesbian youth hotline to ask about coming out. My parents are very religious, very conservative, and the sweet gay boy from the hotline told me to keep quiet until I could move somewhere, shall we say, more sophisticated. Then I should come out."

"She ran away to Frisco the next day," Cassie said, positively schoolgirlish in her admiration.

"Well, the hotline boy didn't say how long I should wait to move, did he?"

"And your mom had no idea why?" I asked.

"Not a stitch," Cassie answered. "Her mom found her and brought her home, but she'd had such a good time in Frisco that she took off again. Next time her mom found her, she'd brought one of the escorts from Red Rock."

"And none of them have any clue why you ran?"

"Clearly not, based upon my roommate situation," Laurel said. "Their ignorance is our bliss." She grinned at Cassie.

"So are you two dears a couple?" the ever-tactful Bebe asked.

"We don't feel the need to define it," Laurel said.

"We ain't a couple," Cassie replied. "But aside from that girl at the beach, Laurel's the first gay person I've ever met."

"Honey, one in ten people are gay," Laurel replied. "I'm just the first queer you *know* you've met."

"Wow, Cass," I said. "They should put you in the brochure. 'I was miserable when I got here, confused about my sexuality. But at Red Rock, I got a lesbian roommate and all my troubles vanished.'"

"It's all too perfect. I must tell Martha. It'll cheer her up. Has anyone seen her?" Bebe asked.

Cassie had seen Martha heading out on one of Sheriff's character-building treks earlier that morning.

"Poor darling," Bebe said. "In this heat."

"I know," Cassie said. "It's hotter than a two-dollar pistol."

"I love it when you talk Texas," Laurel said with an affectionate giggle.

"I guess Brit's not the only one who owes our dear V a nod of thanks," Bebe said, throwing another pointed glance my way.

"Drop it, Bebe," I warned.

"Fine, it's dropped," Bebe said, back to her bitchy voice.

"We'd best split up now," Cassie said. "Don't want to separate the counselors from their *National Enquirer*s."

"*Ciao*, girlies," Bebe said, flittering off.

Cassie and Laurel moved away too. And just like that, I was alone again.

Chapter 20

"Are you ready to talk about your grandmother's letter?" Clayton asked.

"What's to talk about?"

"I really am so tired of your obfuscation, Brit. There's much to discuss in that letter."

"My mom's okay. She's in Spokane. It's all good news."

"Is it really?"

"She's not dead, so relatively speaking, yes it is."

Clayton waved her pen and chuckled softly. This was my cue to ask her what she thought was so funny. "What?" I asked.

Now she was shaking her head. "It's just too obvious."

"If you're going somewhere with this, maybe you should share, because you've lost me."

"I'm not the one who's lost you, Brit," she said. "Let me put it another way. In your grandmother's letter, she said that your mother refused the doctor's help, because she feared they were all, wait, let me get this exactly." She stopped and shuffled through my file, then pulled out a photocopy of Grandma's letter. "She 'thinks the doctors are all out to get her.' Isn't that how you feel?"

"Just because you're paranoid doesn't mean they're not after you," I muttered.

"I beg your pardon?"

"Nothing, a song lyric. I don't think you're trying to poison me or kidnap me so you can plant probes in my brain, which is the kind of stuff my mother believes, if that's what you're getting at."

"You've missed my point. You're being too literal. I'm just suggesting the ways in which your nature mirrors your mother's."

"You keep saying that. Why don't you just ask the

question you're hinting at: Am I worried that I'll go crazy too?"

"To put it bluntly, yes."

"Are your parents still alive, Dr. Clayton?"

"I don't see how that's any of your business."

"Humor me. Is your mom alive?" Clayton was at least fifty so I figured there was a good chance she wasn't.

"My mother is still with us. My father passed on."

"Of what?"

"Where are you taking this, Brit?"

"Just tell me."

"He died of heart disease."

"Are you worried you'll have a heart attack?"

"No more than the next person."

"Well, my mom has a disease, too. That's what all the doctors told Dad and me. It can be hereditary, but my mom's mom is fine and so is her sister, so there's no reason to think I won't be, too." It all sounded so logical. I almost believed it myself.

"That's a very mature way to look at, Brit," Clayton said. "But I suppose that if I had high cholesterol or chest pains and other signs of heart disease, I might change my tune a bit, show a bit more concern, perhaps even try to take some preventive measures."

"Preventive measures, like what? Shock therapy?" I was being sarcastic, but judging by the creepy smile on Clayton's face, I was a little scared that I'd given her an idea.

●   ●   ●

As it turned out, Clayton did have shock treatment in mind for me, but not the kind with electrodes. A couple days later, she called me in for a special session. When I saw who was sitting with her in her office I almost passed out.

Dad.

I was speechless. What was he doing here? Was this the rescue every girl at Red Rock secretly hoped for? Or had something happened to Mom? Clayton took in my confusion, eating it up like candy. Then, after my discomfort had settled over the room, she deigned to explain.

"As you know, Mr. Hemphill, we don't usually condone individual visits, but in Brit's case, I thought we'd make an exception." She turned to me, wearing her phoniest smile. "Your father has generously agreed to give up a day of his family trip to the Grand Canyon to come see if he can't galvanize your therapy."

"You went to the Grand Canyon without me?" Somehow, I felt as betrayed by this as everything else that had happened.

"Yes, honey. It's beautiful there. I wish you could've joined us," Dad replied. I stared at him. Was he for real? I mean, did he think this was a nice social call?

"As I was saying," Clayton interrupted. "Your father agreed to come down for the day to help us work on a few issues." She turned to Dad. "Mr. Hemphill, I think it would help Brit to know exactly how she came to arrive at Red Rock."

Dad nodded and looked at Clayton, who fixed him in a steady gaze. Then he looked at me. It was almost like he was asking for my help to get Clayton out of the room. And because even when I'm furious with Dad I will do anything for him, I cleared my throat. Then Dad cleared his throat. Clayton got the hint.

"Well then, let me give you two some time alone," she said.

Dad stepped forward to hug me. His embrace felt hollow. I extricated myself from it as quickly as I could.

"You were going to tell me why I got sent here," I said, looking squarely at him.

"Your therapists believe you're under the impression that it was your mother's idea."

"My *step*mother's idea," I corrected.

"Right, yes, well. I should clarify now that while she thought you could use some, well, guidance, the decision to send you to Red Rock was mine."

"Your idea?" I spat.

Dad blushed. He actually looked embarrassed. "Yes, your mother—I mean your stepmother—she thought you needed some help dealing with your— your anger, but she was actually against you going so far away," he stammered. "I chose Red Rock. I felt it was the best place for you."

Maybe I'd suspected this all along, but hearing it from Dad's mouth was like a knife in the back. I looked at him, a person I had once loved without limit in this world, and I felt a flash of hatred. It was just for a second, but it cooled my temperature to ice.

"So what sold you on Red Rock?" I asked. "The fact that it's a thousand miles from home? Or was it their warm-and-fuzzy therapeutic approach that appealed to you?"

Not even Dad could miss my sarcasm. He ran his hands through his hair. "Please, sweetheart. We just have a short visit. Let's try to be civil."

"Civil? Do you think that's why Clayton asked you here? For a tea party? She wants you to bring me down a few pegs. Which is how this place operates."

"Now, honey. I'm sure that's not true. I know that Dr. Clayton is stern, but she has your best interests at heart."

It was at that moment that I finally got it: *Dad didn't have a clue.* He didn't have any idea what Red Rock was all about, even though he was standing right in the middle of it and could have seen it for what it was if he'd really wanted to. And maybe more importantly, he didn't have the slightest notion why he'd sent me here. There were so many things I understood that Dad was working diligently to ignore.

"How long are you going to keep doing that?" I asked quietly. "How long are you going to bury your head in the sand?"

Dad looked up at me, as surprised as I was, I guess, by the venom in my voice. "What are you talking about now?" he asked wearily.

I wanted to grab him, to shake him, to wake him up, but I held myself still. "Do you even know why you sent me here? Can you tell me that?" I demanded. Dad stared at me now with the same lost look I recognized from girls in CT.

"Let me enlighten you. You sent me away because you were too powerless to do anything about Mom. So you're trying to compensate with me. You sent me away because you're scared I'm going to . . ."

Dad looked stricken. "I'm scared you're going to what?" he asked.

But I couldn't say it out loud. That would make it real. And hearing Dad confirm it, that would have been more than I could take. Besides, Dad was suddenly looking so ashen that I was scared he was going to pass out or have a heart attack or something. Just like that, my moment of clear-eyed hatred passed, and I was back in a dreary room with my sad sack of a guilt-ridden dad. I felt tears spring to my eyes, but before they had a chance to escape, I left the office.

As I sprinted down the hallway, passing a satisfied-looking Clayton standing just outside the door, I wondered when it was that Dad had become one of the people I had to hide my true self from.

Chapter 21

Dad had finally shown up, he'd admitted that sending me away was his decision, and Clayton seemed hell-bent on convincing me I was a loon: I'd never needed a Sisters meeting so badly in my life. But I didn't even know how to begin to make that happen. The only person who did was locked up.

I was still mad at V. And I still felt guilty. Every day she stayed stuck on Level Two weighed on me. But even with all my conflicting feelings, I missed her. I needed her plainspoken solace now more than ever.

Two days after Dad's visit, I was feeling so riled up that I decided to infiltrate iso and talk to V. On my way to breakfast, I fell in with a large group of Level Three girls, and when they turned toward the cafeteria, I veered off to the wing where the iso rooms were. The halls were empty, and my heart was pounding. I felt like I was being watched from every direction.

At the end of the iso corridor, I spotted two Level Six guards chatting outside what I figured was V's door. I crouched down, trying to psych myself forward. But I couldn't get my legs to work. It wasn't just getting caught or bitched out by the Sixers that scared me. It was facing V. I didn't even know where things stood between us, and besides, she had this way of zeroing in on stuff I didn't want to talk about. Ironically, she was a lot like Clayton that way.

So I chickened out and made my way back to the cafeteria, feeling like a miserable loser. By the time I arrived, most of the girls were getting ready to leave. I spotted Cassie and Laurel together, and Bebe, walking two paces in front of her guard, Hilary, who was carrying both of their trays. That almost made me laugh, and almost made me run up to Bebe, but I couldn't help remembering the time she'd said Dad didn't really want to see me. Even though he'd just visited, Bebe's proclamation seemed truer than ever, and I didn't relish having her rub my face in it. Just when I thought I was totally alone—salvation. I saw Martha. This was a rarity. Martha was hardly ever around these days.

"Oh my God, am I glad to see you, Martha," I said.

She swiveled to face me. She looked exhausted, her face pale, her eyes droopy. "Oh, hey Brit," she said wearily.

"Are you going to school now? I've got to talk to you."

Martha shook her head. "Can't. I have to go on another one of Sheriff's lame overnight hikes," she said. She was practically in tears.

"Do you have five minutes? I'm desperate."

"I wish," she said mournfully. "I'm already in trouble because I overslept. They're waiting for me. I get back tomorrow around lunchtime. I'll find you then." She gave me a helpless shrug and was gone.

The next day, I eagerly looked for Martha in the cafeteria at lunch. She wasn't there. She didn't show up for dinner, either, or for breakfast the next day. I looked for her in school. Not there. She wasn't on the quarry, either. I checked to see if she was in iso or in the infirmary or had been switched to the other class. But she was MIA. I asked Bebe, Cass, and Laurel if they'd seen her, but they hadn't. I was getting so worried that I sought out Tiffany after group therapy.

"Hey Tiff."

She stared at me, her eyes angry slits. It struck me then how much Tiffany disliked me, how much she resented all of the Sisters. Did she know about our secret meetings? Did she feel left out? Maybe we should've invited her.

"What do *you* want?"

"I was just wondering if you'd seen Martha. I haven't seen her in a couple of days. Have you?"

Tiffany looked nervous for a second, and then she actually smiled, like the cat that swallowed the canary.

"What?" I asked

"I'm not allowed to say."

"What aren't you allowed to say?"

"If I told you, I'd be saying it." I felt my fist clench. I so wanted to punch her kiss-assy face. But she had vital information, so I took a breath to steady myself.

"Has she gone home? Is she okay?"

"She hasn't gone home, and she's okay, as okay as

any of you troublemakers are." Now Tiffany was actually gloating.

"Where is she? I'm really worried."

"I'll bet you are," she sneered. "You and your little group. I'm sorry, but I'm just not permitted to tell you anything more." She turned on her heel and was gone.

After my conversation with Tiffany, the bad feeling I'd had blossomed into full-on panic. Something was very wrong. That night at dinner, I found out just how wrong. A Level Five girl named Pam, whom I had never talked to before, sat down next to me.

"I'm not supposed to tell you this, but I'm going to anyway," she said.

Pam started telling me about the most recent death march, the overnight expedition Martha had gone on. Even though the temperature had been in the nineties when the hike started, Sheriff had pushed the girls as usual. As usual, Martha was at the back of the pack. Pam said Martha had been complaining of a headache, but Sheriff just told her "less whining, more climbing," and when Martha kept complaining, he threatened to demote her to Level Three. So she kept going.

"That night Martha said that her head hurt and

her feet felt all tingly," Pam told me. "I could tell she wasn't faking. I started to get worried. And it only got worse. She started to get all spacey. I went to Sheriff's tent and told him about Martha, but he just told me to mind my own business and that she'd be fine in the morning."

"That sounds like him. Was she better?"

"Worse. She could hardly eat the measly breakfast and she seemed really confused and was walking slower than ever. I knew something was seriously wrong, so I hung back with her, just wanting to get her down the mountain and to the infirmary. After breakfast, we started hiking again. It was blazing hot. Martha started to lose it, babbling, and calling me Anita."

"That's her sister's name," I said.

"By then I was really scared, and I ran to get Sheriff. He was totally annoyed but he followed me back to where I'd left Martha, and she'd just kind of crumpled up under a tree. Sheriff thought she was sleeping. He kept yelling at her to wake up, get off her fat ass and stuff like that. But she didn't move."

"Oh my God. Is she okay?"

"I don't know. I'm pretty sure she's still at the hospital now."

"The hospital?" My stomach somersaulted. I was scared that I might throw up.

"That's where they took her. And that was just because we all gathered around Sheriff and Martha and started freaking out and yelling at him until he got on the walkie-talkie. I heard she's been in a coma since then. I'm really sorry to have to tell you this."

My eyes welled up. "Please don't," Pam said, though not unkindly. "We're not supposed to talk about this, and if anyone finds out I told you, I could get in big trouble. Please don't cry."

I wiped my nose and got myself together. "I don't want to get you in trouble," I said. "But they must know we're going to find out what happened to her, what they did."

"They've already figured out how to cover their tracks. You think Red Rock is gonna take the blame for this? No way. They're going to blame Martha. Blame the victim. That should be Red Rock's motto."

That night, I didn't have any problem keeping myself awake until two in the morning. I stole into the hall and when I saw the guard was asleep, I made my way to Bebe's room. "Wake up," I whispered, my hand over Bebe's mouth. I beckoned her to follow me.

"What is it?" she asked.

"Meet me in the office. You get Cassie. I'm going for V."

"But she's under heavy surveillance."

"It doesn't matter. This matters. Ten minutes."

Whereas two days ago I'd crept through these halls like some kind of stalked prey, this time I felt like a lion. I walked purposefully, ducking wherever there was a camera. I grabbed the pass key from its hiding place in the fake plant next to Clayton's office and made my way to V's room. The guard was nowhere to be seen. I knew what I was doing was dangerous, could get me sent back a level or three, delaying my leaving Red Rock for months. But none of that seemed to matter anymore. Dad seemed content to leave me here as long as he could. And Martha needed us.

V seemed to have a sixth sense that I was coming. She was wide awake on her cot, as though expecting me. As soon as she saw me through the window of her door, she slipped out of bed. I unlocked the door, and V fell into step silently next to me. When the group assembled, I told them what I had heard just a few hours ago, what the staff at Red Rock was so desperately trying to cover up.

"Martha's in the hospital. In a coma," I said. The girls all gasped in horror. And then I told them everything Pam had told me at dinner, plus a few things I'd found out since then. What I didn't tell them about was Dad. Suddenly it no longer seemed relevant.

"Get this, you know why Sheriff says Martha passed out?" I asked.

"Heat stroke, dehydration, exhaustion," V suggested.

"Those would be the obvious reasons. No, he's telling everyone that Martha is anorexic and has been starving herself for weeks now."

"That is such a load of crap," V said.

"Of course it is. But rat-fink Tiffany backed him up. She told Pam that she'd seen Martha hiding food in her sock and Tiffany told Sheriff that too. So now he's telling everyone who asks that Martha is a victim of malnourishment because she's been withholding food. There's going to be an announcement tomorrow at breakfast."

"That's such a load of bull," Cassie fumed. "They did this to her. It ain't right."

It was worse than not right. It was cruel. I kept picturing poor Martha, slowly losing it on the hike and no one listening to her, no one trusting her, because what? She was a formerly thin girl who'd dared to get fat? What had any of us done to belong here? Cassie liked girls too much. Bebe liked boys too much. V thought of death too much. And me? Why was I here? Because I resembled my mom too much? Because I scared my dad too much?

Seeing what happened to Martha, how the school reacted to it, I finally got it. Who was screwed up—Martha, or her thin-obsessed parents? Cassie, or her homophobic mom and dad? V, or her too-busy-to-care power parents? Me, or my willfully deluded father? As I sat there and thought everything through, something sparked in me. I'd hated Red Rock from the get-go but never knew what to do about it. I relied on V to help me break rules, or Bebe to help me outwit Clayton, or Jed to fill my mind with happy thoughts. But like a volcano burbling, something was coming alive in me. Not just anger but indignation, and a new resolve. I was tired of being in the charge of cruel and clueless adults. The world was upside down. The adults had abandoned their roles. They'd surrounded themselves in a cocoon of ignorance—and then told us we were screwed up. We couldn't trust them anymore. There was nobody out there watching out for us, taking care of us. We had to look out for ourselves.

And to do that, I had to change. Because in spite of Dad and Clayton's mischaracterizations, in spite of my punky hair and tattoos and affinity for guitar feedback, I was basically a good girl. I had listened to my parents when I had two of them, and listened to my dad when Mom left. I was nice enough to Billy. I didn't take drugs or drink or steal or hurt people. I was honest and I could love people and be loved. I wasn't the rebellious girl the Red Rock staff liked to paint me as. But I realized that if I wanted to get out and get my life back, I was going to have to become *that* girl. It was time to awaken my inner rebel, time to kick some ass.

"It's all so awful, my poor sweet girl," Bebe lamented.

"I hate these people," V said. "How can they be so venal? They're supposed to be helping us, and look what they do? They undermine us and hurt us in the name of therapy."

"You're statin' the obvious, but what can we do, short of organizing a prison break?" Cassie asked.

"Enough," I interrupted.

"Sorry," Cassie said, raising her hands. "I was just thinkin' out loud."

"No, not you. Enough of them. Enough of this bullshit therapy. Enough of waiting for Clayton and Sheriff to decide when we're fixed. Enough of our parents with their heads in the sand, warehousing us here while they ignore their own problems. The rules just changed. What we say, what we do—it's not up to them anymore. It's up to us. Game over."

"I like this vigilante talk, darling. Tell us what you have in mind," Bebe said, looking at me for the first time in ages with warmth, like the old Bebe.

"Yeah, what's your plan?" V asked.

"I'll tell you my plan: The end of Red Rock. For everyone. We're going to shut this place down."

Chapter 22

Two nights later, I found myself sneaking through the halls again. Even though I'd snuck out at night before and had used the pass key myself a couple of times, every nerve in my body was on high alert. I could almost feel Sheriff's hand clamping on my shoulder, but I kept going. When I got to the administrative offices, I opened the door. Shimmying on my belly to avoid being filmed, I made my way over to the phone and pulled it onto the floor. Lying on my back, my hands shaking, I dialed Ansley and Beth's number. It was two o'clock in the morning, and I thought for sure they'd be home. But the machine picked up.

"Hi guys. This is Brit, over at Red Rock. I'm sorry

to call so late, but remember how you said you wanted to get this place shut down? Well, so do we. And I need your help. I'll try to call back in a few days. I'm afraid it'll have to be late, but please try to answer your phone."

I hung up and was about to head back to the room when on impulse, I dialed Jed. Not my lucky night. I got his machine too, but just to hear his soft rumbly voice, it gave me the chills. "Jed, it's Brit. Are you there? Pick up. Look, I'm sorry I haven't been able to write you. It's not that I don't think about you because I do, always, and I'm going to get out of here and we can be together so please hang in there, because Jed, you're my firefly too." I paused, listening to the line crackle, feeling like I was standing at the edge of a cliff. And then I threw myself over. "I love you, " I whispered into the machine. "I needed to tell you that." Then I hung up, and crawled back to my bed, giddy and scared with the knowledge that I had just set two balls in motion.

Three nights later, I was creeping through the halls again, praying that I wouldn't get caught. This time, Beth and Ansley were home. They were delighted to hear from me, although not exactly brimming with the best of advice. They seemed to watch too many movies, because most of their suggestions were completely unrealistic. They recommended blowing up the school or digging out a tunnel or torturing the staff. Um . . . I'd seen *Heathers* and *Shawshank Redemption* and *Breakfast Club*, but no thanks. I listened to all their ridiculous ideas and thanked them, but asked for something more low-key, along the lines of getting a civil rights attorney, a congressman, or a journalist involved.

"Sorry, Brit. St. George isn't really the center of the Utah political scene. That's up north, and they're all pretty conservative Mormons," Ansley said.

"What about going to the local paper?" I asked

"Again, this is a pretty small town. Front-page stories are usually about new construction or record-breaking weather," Beth explained.

"It doesn't have to be here. We could write to another paper or something. Or call," I said.

Over the phone line, I heard Beth suck in her breath. "What?" Ansley and I asked in unison.

"What about Skip Henley?" Beth asked.

"Who?" I said.

"Oh, I don't know, Beth," Ansley said.

"Who's Kip Henley?"

"*Skip* Henley. He's a pretty famous journalist. He

covered Vietnam. Nixon. Watergate. He's kind of ancient. But he was a hotshot in his day. He won a Pulitzer Prize. Left his job about ten years ago. It was a big hubbub. He wrote some exposé about government defense contracts and refused to reveal his sources. He had to go to court and ended up being put in jail for contempt. Something like that."

"He quit his job in protest. It was a major story. And he's been retired ever since. Occasionally he gives a talk about world affairs at the local college," Ansley said, "but mostly he just raises horses at his ranch."

"He sounds perfect," I said.

"He's notoriously cranky," Ansley warned.

"Get me his number."

• • •

A week later, my hands quaking, I called the number Beth had given me. It was one o'clock and I knew I'd probably wake him, but better Henley than the guard. By the gruff tenor of his voice, however, it was clear that even though he was awake, calls at this late hour were not okay.

"Mr. Henley," I began, my voice quavering.

"Who the hell is this, and why in God's name are you calling at this hour?"

"I'm sorry it's so late. My name's Brit Hemphill. I'm a student, well more like an inmate, really, at Red Rock Academy. It's near you."

"Is this a prank? I'm hanging up."

"No, please don't hang up. I go to this school, it's really a boot camp for teens. They do horrible things here, really awful. I thought you might want to do a story."

"I'm retired. Leave me alone."

"I know you are, but I just don't—I don't know what else to do. Someone has to listen to us," I said, my voice breaking off.

"You damn kids. Get a life." Then he hung up.

I snuck back into my room, climbed into bed, and threw myself a pity party. Screw Skip Henley. No one was ever going to listen. But as I was feeling sorry for myself, I heard Jed's voice in my head, and I so wanted to be the rock star he seemed to think I was. That's why the next night, I called again.

The second time, at least, Henley listened to my spiel. And then he laughed. "Kid, do you know who I am?"

"Yeah, you're famous for covering a bunch of stuff

in the seventies, right?"

"Do your homework, kid. I've covered wars, revolutions, assassinations. And you want me to tell the world about a bunch of whiny rich kids who think their school's too tough?"

"It's not like that."

Henley chuckled again. "Maybe next I can do an exposé on the price-gouging of lip gloss." Then, still laughing, he hung up.

• • •

This was going to be tougher than I thought. But I wasn't about to give in. I called another meeting with the Sisters and explained what I'd been doing.

"You're crazy, darling. And I love you for it," Bebe said.

"This does kick it up a level," Cassie said.

"I know, but it's not working. He laughed at me."

"Never trust anyone over thirty," Cassie said. "I'm beginnin' to think those are words to live by."

"But I feel like he's our best hope," I said. "I mean, what are the chances of a big-time investigative journalist living out here? If we can just get him to believe us. To make the case."

"So make the case," V said. She looked at me with that same mix of exasperation and helpfulness she had back when I was on Level One and was stubbornly refusing to tell Sheriff that I was ready to face myself.

"How?"

"My dad had a bunch of hotshot journalist friends," V said. "All they care about is a juicy story. They can smell it like blood. You've just got to show him it's a good story."

I looked at her. She was offering help, but there was that coldness again. It had been that way since she'd gotten off Level Two, since I'd come up with my plan, since she'd told me to hold on to the pass key and said it was time for me to be the keeper of the flame for a while. I couldn't tell if she knew that I was still kinda mad at her or if she was jealous that it was me leading this charge and not her. Maybe she didn't want there to be any charge at all.

* * *

Another night, another break-in. This time it was the computer room, where Level Sixers were allowed to send email. Only staff knew the log-in code. Ansley and Beth had told me that when they were at Red Rock, the code had been—oh so imaginatively—*teenhelp*, and I was sure they would've changed it. But never underestimate the laziness of Red Rock. Because when the password box popped up and I typed in TEENHELP—expecting the computer to immediately crash or a siren to go off—Internet Explorer opened up and I heard the modem dial and connect. Bingo.

I spent almost an hour googling. First I looked up Skip Henley. I was so embarrassed. Not only had he done a bunch of amazing stories in the seventies, but since then, he'd covered lots of human-rights stuff, the death squads in Nicaragua, the Truth and Reconciliation Commission in South Africa. He was as famous a journalist as Walter Cronkite, and I'd disrespected him. That wasn't going to happen again.

Then I googled Red Rock. I didn't get much, mostly the school's own website. So I googled Dr. Clayton and then Bud "Sheriff" Austin, and found nothing. I was about to give up, but then I googled "Austin," "former sheriff" and "boot camp" and got this, from the *Billings Gazette*:

BOYS' BOARDING SCHOOL CLOSED
FOR INVESTIGATION

A local school has been shut, amid allegations of child abuse and civil rights infringements. Authorities say that they are continuing to investigate Piney Creek, a private boarding school that bills itself as a boot camp for out-of-control teen boys. Former students and local activists have long claimed that the school's tactics, including restraining students with handcuffs, placing them in isolation, and withholding food, amount to cruel and unusual punishment. "These young men have not been charged with any crime by the criminal justice system, and yet they receive fewer rights and harsher treatment than they would in prison," says local lawyer Sharon Michner, who represents a family suing the school after

their son suffered scabies and malnutrition. "There is an astonishing lack of state or federal control of these institutions, and that leads to widespread abuse."

Piney Creek principal Arnold "Bud" Austin, a former sheriff, declined comment, but the school issued a written statement. "With school shootings and teen violence up, we need to broaden our arsenal in reclaiming young people who have gone down the wrong path. We have helped hundreds of young men, and the allegations made against Piney Creek are baseless."

Police Chief Richard Hall said the school will remain closed and the students will return to their families or transfer to new schools until the investigation is complete.

I found two more articles from the *Gazette*, one announcing that the investigation was complete and the school was closed for good, and another noting that Michner's case had been settled out of court for an undisclosed sum. After that, I googled "Arnold Austin" and "boot camp" and hit pay dirt. Turned out, Sheriff had been in charge of at least three other schools, one in Idaho, one in Utah, and one in Jamaica. Both the Idaho and the Utah schools had been shut down by authorities.

How was it that Piney Creek was shuttered but Red Rock could still be open? How was it that Sheriff's schools had been deemed abusive over and over, but he was still in business? I didn't have any answers, but I did know one thing: I had a story. And Skip Henley was going to have one too.

When I crawled back into my room that night, Missy was wide awake in her bed.

"Where have *you* been?" she asked, shocking the hell out of me. The one good thing about having her as a roommate was that she was a deep sleeper.

"Bathroom," I answered.

"For forty-five minutes?"

"I ate the creamed chipped beef tonight," I lied, clutching my stomach. "Big mistake." Missy glared at me. "If you don't believe me, you can go to the bathroom. It still stinks pretty bad in there."

"That won't be necessary," she harrumphed before rolling over and going back to sleep. I'd been dodging so many bullets with all my sneaking around that week, I couldn't help but worry that my luck would run out.

• • •

The next day on the quarry, I told the Sisters what I had found. V, who I'd thought would be more supportive, just said, "Well done." I wasn't sure she meant it. Bebe, Cassie, and Laurel, on the other hand, practically peed with excitement.

"Now Skip's got to hear you out," Cassie said. "You've hit the mother lode."

"You did some pretty good digging there," Laurel added.

"Pretty good?" Bebe swooned. "You're brilliant, and so sly."

"Well not that sly. I almost got caught by Missy. I don't know how much I can risk sneaking out again. I can't have diarrhea every night."

"Gross, darling," Bebe said. "That's a tad too much information."

"I think I should wait a week until I try contacting Henley again," I said.

"You could get one of us to help," Laurel suggested.

"Oh please, let me," Bebe offered. "Hilary's so dumb I can tell her anything. I'll join the Mission Impossible and call good old Skip myself. Besides, it would feel nice to do something for Martha. It has to beat being miserable and waiting for news."

"I know. All the silence is driving me crazy. Any word?" I asked.

"Nothing yet. Status quo," V said. "She's still in the hospital, as far as I know."

We were all silent for a second, thinking of Martha. "Okay, then," Bebe announced. "So who is this geezer I'm supposed to charm?"

"Skip Henley. He's a really big-time reporter," I

said. "And you don't need to charm him, just convince him."

"I'll do both. I'll have him eating out of my hands. You know I was interviewed by Joan Rivers with Mother? Once you've tussled with that broad, you can handle virtually anyone."

• • •

As it turned out, Bebe couldn't handle Skip Henley. She called him two nights later and before she could even start with her evidence, he interrupted her.

"God, he was so rude," Bebe complained. "At first I thought he was going to help, because he asked the name of the school and the principal. So I told him, and he growled into the phone that if I ever called again, he would alert the school. Then he started railing on about what a bunch of—let me see if I can remember it—'spoiled, entitled, apathetic babies,' our generation was, how we never get up in arms about anything except the latest Xbox game. Like I'd waste my time with video games. Please." Bebe stopped. She turned to me. "Sorry Brit, but I think we're barking up the wrong tree with this guy. He's a bitter old pill. Worse than Joan."

"It was a valiant effort. Too bad it didn't work out," V said. I'd never have thought that she, of all people, would give up on us so quickly.

"Yeah, Brit," Bebe added. "It was a good try. But it's really an impossible deed you're trying to accomplish."

I was disappointed by how readily the Sisters were all giving up, but not all that surprised. Red Rock was designed to make us doubt ourselves. It was how the school broke us, got us to submit to the program. But I wasn't ready to give up. I needed to talk to someone who believed in me. I needed to talk to Jed.

Except that I hadn't heard from Jed since the night I left that stupid message on his machine. After a few days, the excitement I'd felt at admitting I loved him was clouded by doubt. What if I'd blown it, said too much, shown my hand? I wasn't much of a game player with guys, and Jed and I had been such good friends that it hadn't occurred to me to be anyone but me. I didn't totally regret what I'd done because I believe in telling the truth, but I tried to imagine what it must have been like to get that message—hearing my desperate voice in the dark. After two weeks and no word from Jed, I figured I had my answer. I'd over-stepped, scared him. Sure, Jed was amazing, but he was also a guy, and guys are skittish about love. Aren't they?

Chapter 23

May turned into June. I turned seventeen and told no one. I got a card from Dad and hoped to get one from Jed, until I realized he didn't know when my birthday was. The days were so hot, over a hundred degrees. Sheriff even canceled backcountry therapy. A kind of tired malaise settled over the Sisters. Restrictions had eased, but not enough so we could really hang out. The big plan had stalled. It was all just blah. The only bright spots on the horizon were two pieces of good news we got in early June. First of all, Cassie's graduation date was set for August. And then there was Martha.

Martha had recovered and was going home. Best

yet, her mom and dad were bringing her by Red Rock to get her stuff, get checked out, and say good-bye to us. I was surprised that they were going to allow her and her parents on campus and shocked when Bebe, V, Cassie, and I got pulled from lunch to attend a private farewell meeting in the front parking lot. And then I was completely speechless when I saw Martha: She had lost at least thirty pounds.

After we all hugged and wiped our eyes, Martha laughed. "Can you believe it? After everything, Red Rock accomplished what it was supposed to. Made me skinny."

"It's true, darling, but you look awful!"

"Bebe!" V scolded. But as usual, Bebe was just telling the truth. Martha had big, dark circles under her eyes, and her rosy complexion had a sallow tint. Her skin also seemed to kind of hang off her where she'd lost the most weight.

"Give me a break. I was in a coma. They tried to tell my mom that I was anorexic. But she knows me too well, knows how much I like to eat. I had kidney failure caused by severe dehydration. Who knew getting hot could do such damage?" Martha said, beckoning us all into a huddle. "Mom's furious at this place," she whispered. "She yelled at Sheriff. She's got them scared, so they're kissing her butt. That's why they let me have this meeting with you, to say 'bye."

"Your mom's not the only one," Cassie said, pointing to me. "This girl was livid. She's been on a campaign to get this place closed down."

"Yeah, except it kind of fizzled," I said.

Martha stared at me, her eyes shining. "Don't give up, Brit. Don't. If anyone can do it, you can. Please don't give up. Please?"

"Okay. Okay. Take it easy," I said.

"I'm sorry. It's just that you guys kept me going in here and I can't bear the thought of leaving you behind." Martha started to cry.

"Darling, what is it?" Bebe asked.

"I don't know. I just feel so, I can't explain it, like everything's whooshing around inside me. I'm so sad to leave you."

"You're not leaving us," I said. "You're going home. There's a difference."

"Yeah. What's the first thing you're gonna do back home?" Cassie asked.

"I don't know. Eat. My mom's dying to put some

weight back on me. Isn't that hilarious?"

"She wants you fat again?" Bebe asked incredulously.

"She wants me healthy."

"We all do," V said.

"Thanks, V. So everything's okay with you all. I mean you and Brit aren't still mad at each other?"

"Brit and I were mad at each other?" V asked, raising her eyebrows. "Or was it that Brit was mad at me?" she said, giving me one of her intense, I-can-see-your-soul stares.

"Oh God, I put my foot in it. As usual. I'm sorry— please don't fight. It makes me sad."

"Everything's fine, Martha," I said.

"Please get out soon. So you can come visit me. I'll make you icebox cake," Martha said, smiling at me and Bebe.

"And lemonade, darling."

"And lemonade. And I'll catch you a firefly."

"No, don't catch it. Just say hi to one for me."

Martha's mom tooted the horn. "Okay. I think I gotta go now. I'm going to miss you guys so much."

"We'll miss you, too. But we'll see you again," V said. "You can bet on that."

"Brit's gonna make sure of it. Aren't you?" Martha said.

All I could do was agree. We hugged Martha one last time and watched as she climbed into the back of her parents' rental car and zoomed back to her old life.

• • •

After Martha left, I felt renewed in my purpose. But I found it hard to get anyone else on board. Bebe was over Henley. She now preferred to organize a letter-writing campaign to her senator. V was still acting weirdly aloof about the whole thing. And Cassie—well, she was off in her own world concentrating on Laurel and her own pending graduation. I couldn't blame her. She was so close to freedom. Why blow it? Only V would do that.

Henley's reaction had taken a bit of the wind out of my sails too, but I wasn't going to give up. I just needed a new game plan. The Sisters were convinced Henley wasn't going to come around, but I still thought he was our best hope. I needed a pep talk, so I decided to risk another outing to call Jed. It was after two o'clock in the morning, but he picked up right away.

"Hello."

"Brit?"

"Yeah, it's me. Um . . . how are you?"

Jed let out a long sigh on the other end of the line. I could practically see him smiling and shaking his head, could picture the exact curve of the lips I'd kissed. "I'm better now. But you had me worried. I've been in Massachusetts the past two weeks and I came home to your one message and nothing else. I thought you freaked out on me or you got into trouble. Are you in trouble?"

"I've pretty much been in trouble since I got here."

"Wanna tell me about it now?"

And so I did, as fast as I could, because the clock was ticking. I told him about what had happened after I'd slipped out to meet him. I told him what happened to Martha and what I'd discovered and what I'd tried and failed to do.

"I don't know, Jed. This Henley guy, he's a jerk, but he's the real deal. I feel like if I could just show him what's happening here, show him what I'm really trying to do . . ."

"Do it," Jed interrupted.

"What?"

"Don't give up. Do whatever it takes to get that place shut down. I'll help you if I can. But I think you're all you need, Brit. It's up to you."

"You think so?"

" I know so, and besides . . ."

"What?"

"I need you to get out," he said, his voice softening. "The real you. I've been carrying on with the fantasy for years now."

"Don't you mean months? It was only March when we, you know, got together . . ."

"I mean years."

"Oh." I just sat there like an idiot, smiling into the phone.

"Can you call me again?"

"Maybe, but they probably go over the long-distance bills with a magnifying glass."

"Call collect then. And get out of there. Clod needs you. Seriously. If you don't get out of there soon, I'm going to turn into a total sap. You'll understand when you hear the songs I've been writing. All ballads."

"Yikes. I'm surprised Erik and Denise haven't staged an intervention." I paused, took a breath. "I miss you."

"Me too. And Brit?"

"Yes?"

"I love you, too."

Okay, maybe he wasn't a typical skittish boy after all.

•   •   •

The Sisters and I met a few nights later, and I laid it out for them. I told them I wanted to give it one more shot with Henley, to present him with the whole story. He didn't even know about Sheriff's history, and there was probably plenty more dirt where that came from. But it was up to us to unearth it. After all, who knew Red Rock better than we did? We would sneak out files, snoop through offices, catalog every inmate's diagnosis. And then, when we had an airtight case, we'd take it to Henley. He'd believe us. He had to.

"I don't know why you're so hung up on this old journalist," Bebe said. "He's such a rude man."

"I've just got a feeling. I mean, if you knew the

guy's history—he's done all this work to expose injustice. He's got to have a big heart under all that gruffness, or at least he used to."

I explained what I felt we needed to do. Cassie, because she was getting out soon, would have to have the least risky job. She'd do an informal survey, find out what every girl at Red Rock was in for. How many sexual deviants, how many kleptos, druggies, or none of the aboves. And how many girls were on medication.

"Be careful, Cassie. Don't take any risks."

"I got it covered, Brit."

I assigned Bebe to get into the medical files—find out how many girls might have had suspicious "accidents" like Martha's or been sick. We needed a list of cases that stunk of typical Red Rock staff neglect.

I gave V what I thought was the second-hardest job: Getting the goods on the staff and finding out how many of them didn't even have the minimum qualifications to dole out advice and meds. She rolled her eyes. "Please, that'll take me all of five seconds. What else you got?"

"The insurance part. If we can prove that Red Rock 'cures' girls as soon as their insurance runs out if their families can't keep paying, that will help make our case."

"Done. And what are you doing?"

"I'm going to break into Clayton's office. Get our files. Compare notes. See if they're making stuff up. And I'm also going to go online, or have Jed do it, to find some graduates who can tell their own torrid tales. I'll bet there are a lot of girls out there who would happily spill their guts about this place."

"It all sounds a mite dangerous," Cassie said.

"I'm afraid so, darling," Bebe agreed. "You know I love the whole Mission Impossible idea, but however are we going to get access to all this stuff? You act like we can just waltz around wherever we please."

I was beginning to understand that we could do just that. I didn't want to risk the girls getting busted, especially Cassie, but in my few nights of sneaking around, my confidence had been growing. Red Rock had us all so scared, so convinced that they were lurking around every corner, that we all stayed in line (at least most of the time). But the reality was that Big Brother was mostly in our heads. Red Rock had some half-assed security system, and one measly nap-loving guard at night. The Sisters had been sneaking out for meetings for almost a year and no one was any the wiser. I'd been caught when I broke out, but that wasn't because any of the staff had nabbed me so much as that someone on the outside had seen me in my uniform and called Sheriff. I was starting to realize that the most effective restraint at Red Rock wasn't the locked doors or the alarms, but our own fear. And only we could unlock that. I tried to explain that to the girls, but at the same time, I didn't want my theory to be their downfall. Cassie and Bebe still looked a little dubious, but it was V who stepped up and saved me.

"Brit, congratulations. You have just discovered the secret of this place." She had a sad look on her face, but I could see that it was tinged with pride.

"I have?" I asked.

"You have. The only thing we have to fear—okay, maybe not the only thing, but the biggest thing we have to fear, with props to FDR—is fear itself."

Bebe took in a gulp of breath. "Oh, what the hell. I'll infiltrate that infirmary if I have to break my leg to do it."

"I'm in too," Cassie said. "And I'll get Laurel to

play sidekick. She works in the office and can make us photocopies if we need 'em."

"I thought you and Laurel were *already* playing sidekick," Bebe teased, making Cassie blush as she turned to me. "See, Brit? We've got your back."

"It's down to you, V," I said.

V stared at me, and then the stern mask of her face broke into a sad smile. "Of course, I'm in. There's no question."

"So, darling," Bebe asked. "What happens once we've dug up all the dirt we need?"

I had no idea. But I figured by the time we got there—if we got there—I'd figure it out.

Chapter 24

For the next two weeks, the four of us were a hive of activity. We hardly saw one another except to check in, share what we'd found, and stash evidence in a hole that Cassie had dug on the edge of the quarry. All of us were totally invigorated—giddy even—the happiest we'd been since we thought we were getting a spa day with Bebe's mom all those months ago. Except no one else could take *this* excitement away from us because we were generating it ourselves. Unless, of course, we got caught.

But we didn't get caught, even as we grew more brazen. Bebe successfully called on her acting lineage and faked an epic case of stomach flu, willing herself to barf. "All I have to do is think about the time we were driving in Mexico and my brother puked on me—I just start to go," Bebe said. "I think Mother would call that method acting." She ended up spending three unaccompanied nights in the infirmary, where no one bothered to lock the files, and she left there, cured, with a bunch of names: In addition to Martha Wallace, there were Gretchen Campbell, Natalie Wiseman, and Hope Ellis. Each of the girls had suffered a suspicious setback. Gretchen had broken her leg, Natalie had come down with scurvy, and someone—the file didn't say who—had broken Hope's nose. We couldn't be sure that any of it had to do with Red Rock's neglect, because Helga, the awful nurse who cavity-searched me, wasn't exactly writing down "student suffered broken nose after fighting with a counselor," but Bebe said that in a lot of cases you could read between the lines. Like scurvy. That could easily have come from a vitamin deficiency brought on by Red Rock's horrendously unbalanced meal plan. And heat stroke? It wasn't hard to imagine girls like Martha being forced to stay in the quarry or complete a death march when conditions were unreasonably hot.

V, in that mysterious way of hers, had managed to get all sorts of goods on the staff. None of the counselors had advanced degrees. Two of them weren't even through college. One of the goon guards used to be a pro wrestler, and another goon had supposedly had his license revoked for drunk driving.

"How did you find out all this stuff?" I asked her. "Are you hypnotizing people, or something?"

"I just ask, Brit. When you give them half a chance people love to talk about themselves, *and each other*."

"Really? I was starting to think you practiced voodoo."

"Not at all. I'm just all smoke and mirrors, like the security system here. I walk into a place like I have a right to be there, and people treat me like I have a right to be there. I act like I have a right to know something, and people tell me what I want to know."

I thought about that. Just act like you had a right to be there. I wondered if I could psych myself into breaking into Clayton's office. Breaking in there and getting our files was the big task I'd set for myself, but so far I hadn't been able to bring myself to do it. There was no camera in Clayton's office, and her file cabinet wasn't locked—just the door was, and I had the pass key. But it felt like the walls had eyes, like they knew everything that happened even in the dark. Just like Clayton seemed to know what happened in the dark recesses of my mind. Why else would she keep harping on about me and Mom, wanting me to accept the possibility that I was going to end up like her? That the qualities I'd inherited from my mother were really just a stop on the road to madness? Part of me thought I should just own up to it. Otherwise, I'd be stuck on Level Four forever. And maybe if Clayton's theory was completely bogus, I would've pretended to agree with her by now. But I wasn't so sure it was, and I was terrified that admitting it to her would only make it real.

So I put off breaking into her office and helped Cassie and Jed follow up on former inmates instead. I'd put Jed in charge of tracking down blogs, diaries, or diatribes from Red Rock graduates. He was on the job, happy to be able to help. It felt good to have him on board. He'd found a bunch of stuff and had emailed links to a secret email account we set up. I checked it as much as I could, but it was Cassie, who took computer classes, who insisted on checking our email account the most. This was pretty risky to do right in front of the counselors, but Cassie insisted on doing more. She'd had a shockingly easy time with her survey. Even the most circumspect girls opened up to her—even the Stockholm syndrome girls, who tended to look down on the nonbelievers like us, told Cassie what she wanted to know. Maybe it was because she was leaving, or maybe because everyone knew by now that Cassie couldn't hurt a fly and wasn't one to spill a secret.

I let Cassie be our computer girl until she almost got caught. One day in class, when she was printing out an email Jed had forwarded, one of the counselors snuck up behind her at her terminal. "I thought my goose was cooked," Cassie told all of us at one of our late-night meetings.

"What did you do, darling?" Bebe asked.

"I hit the powerstrip on my computer, unplugged the whole thing and prayed. Ain't nothin' anyone could do. I mean a smart counselor might've checked my cache on Explorer, but the counselors here are all hat, no cattle if you know what I mean. Still, I was in a panic they'd see what I'd printed. Trust me, it was a long forty-five minutes."

"I'm glad you didn't get caught, but that's enough

Nancy Drew for you, Cassie. You can do more for us on the outside," I said.

"I s'pose you're right. I wouldn't wanna get this close only to blow it."

"No, you wouldn't," I said, sneaking a glance at V.

After that, I took over the email correspondence. Through Jed I found a guy who'd sued Piney Creek, and he emailed that he would happily tell horror stories about Sheriff, including one about a time when Sheriff lassoed him to a chair and sat him in the sun all day. I also got a note from a girl named Andrea who'd been sent to Red Rock ostensibly for drinking. She wrote me that the real reason she'd been sent away was that her parents were fighting for custody of her, and her mom had enrolled her at Red Rock to keep her away from her dad. In the end, her father had to hire a lawyer to get her out. "We've both got lots of sordid things to say about Red Rock and would love to talk to you or whoever else wants to hear about it. I loathe that place with all of my being," she wrote.

I printed out all these emails and stashed them, along with Cassie's printouts and her survey, Bebe's infirmary records, and V's staff notes, in our secret hole by the quarry. After almost two weeks, we had quite the pile going.

"But our little dossier is missing one important element," V said. "Brit, when are you going to get our files?"

"Tonight."

"You said that last night."

"I know. But Missy was restless. It was too dangerous."

"You want me to go?"

"No, V. I can handle it."

"Then do it, already. You got everyone all riled up with this. You can't turn back now."

"By tomorrow morning," I said, "I'll have the files."

•   •   •

I never made it that night. As I lay in my bed, singing Clash songs in my head for inspiration, I told myself it was because of Missy. She was restless again. It was too dangerous to get caught this late in the game. Missy *was* a little restless, going to the bathroom a couple of times, but I could've gone if I'd wanted to, if I'd had the guts.

The next morning, Bebe sidled up to me in the cafeteria, dropped a note on my tray and left.

> *V got caught in Clayton's office last night. Missy told Sheriff that you'd been sneaking around, so they did a stakeout. V's back on Level One. They might press charges against her! I saw her in the bathroom. She said she hid the pass key in her slipper while they questioned her, and then hid it back in the plant. She said to tell you that she is sorry. What now? Are we screwed?*

It was the second time V had taken the fall for me. And once again, I was angry. But this time it was me I was pissed at. I'd allowed V to claim responsibility for my breakout and now I'd hesitated in following through with my grand plan. V didn't hesitate. She marched into risk. And willingly paid the price for it.

Right there in the cafeteria I made a decision: I would go into Clayton's office, not that night, when everyone would be looking, but that day. I would go in because I had a right to be there, and the walls were only plaster and brick. I would get our files. I would make copies of them during dinner and I'd have them back before dark. Soon they'd change the key or lock the files or do something to keep one of us from striking again. Now was my window, and I had to leap through before it closed.

Clayton saw students in the morning and then again in the late afternoon, and she left Red Rock in between. I just had to sneak off the quarry and into her office, hide the files somewhere for Laurel to copy, and replace the originals, with no one the wiser. It was the equivalent of a commando mission behind enemy lines in broad daylight, with no camouflage and no backup. But it was what I had to do.

As soon as the door clicked closed behind me, I shuddered. Even though the rest of Red Rock had lost much of its intimidating veneer, Clayton's office still had an ominous atmosphere. It felt like she was there, looking over my shoulder, though I'd checked to make sure her car was gone. I hated Clayton's office more than any other room at Red Rock. It was like a cave housing all my deepest fears. I took a deep breath and reached for her file cabinet. It was unlocked.

An odd calm came over me as I went through the files, plucking out WALLACE, JONES, LARSON, HOWARTH, and finally, HEMPHILL. I knew I had to work fast—get in, get out—but holding my file in my hand, I couldn't resist. I flipped it open, and phrases like "denial" "idealizing iconoclastic characteristics," "narcissism" "in common with mother," "paranoid schizophrenia" glared at me in Clayton's neat print. There was also a sheaf of Xeroxed letters my dad and grandma had sent, including some from Jed. And then there was a letter I'd never seen. It wasn't a copy. It was the original, on what looked like a brown paper bag in handwriting I knew all too well. I dropped the rest of the files and sank to the floor.

My dearest, darling ever-lasting lovey Brit:
    There are some mornings I wake up and it's almost like I've forgotten the years that have passed. I see you so clearly—you in your pajamas, twirling scarves on the lawn, your feet wet with morning dew. You're just a blur of color, all brightness and joy. I'm inside, making breakfast,

watching you, thinking, how is it that I made this? How is it that this came from me? Call it life, call it a miracle. I just call it you, my biggest and best contribution to the world.

I'm so sorry for everything that's happened. I'm so sorry for being taken away from you. I count it a blessing that most of the time I don't even know I'm sorry. But every so often comes a day like this when the chase stops, and for a moment, I'm free. It's like at home in the winter, when just for a day, the gray goes away, and the sky is so clear you can see the mountain perfectly. Today is one of those days.

It won't last. The clouds always return to the sky and my own clouds come back to reclaim me. But I write this for you now as a testament—a sign that I was here, that I was your mom once, that I still am.

When I finished reading, my tears were blinding me and I'd dampened the letter. I couldn't see, I couldn't hear, I couldn't move. But then it was like some invisible force pulled me out of that office, away from the dark room where all my worst fears lived.

That same force guided me through the rest of the day. I don't know how else to explain the way I managed to stash the files under my mattress, go back to the quarry, tell Laurel to make the copies, act halfway normal, get the files back from Laurel before dinner, and after dinner return the originals to Clayton's office. Especially on this of all days, when V's break-in had everyone up in arms again and acting all top-security. It was like someone else was leading me; it took me a while to understand that that someone else had really been the strongest part of me.

I hadn't meant to read anyone else's files. The plan had been to distribute each one to its subject and let the girls annotate their own, separating the truth from Red Rock's lies. And really, all I wanted was for Missy to fall asleep so I could read my file again, read Mom's letter again. I figured Grandma must have found Mom's note and sent it to me. But why had Clayton chosen not to show it to me? To protect me? To punish me?

When the lights went out and I cracked our door to read by the glow of the hall, V's papers were on top.

And on the top of her file was her date of birth. V was Aquarius, born in February. At first I didn't give it a second thought, and I put her stuff on the bottom to get back to my own file. But then I looked back at her year of birth and I did the math. V was eighteen. She'd been eighteen for months—which meant she could've checked herself out ages ago. And I don't know why, but the truth about V made me cry almost as hard as seeing my mom's letter.

Chapter 25

"I want to speak to Virginia."

It was the next morning, and after breakfast, instead of going to school, I had walked over to the isolation rooms where V was being kept. Once upon a time, I'd have been frightened to go over there, but, ironically, V's own words egged me on: *Act like you have a right to be there. Act like you have a right to know the answers.*

"You can't talk to her. She's on Level One," replied the annoying Level Sixer sitting outside the room.

"I wasn't asking your permission," I said.

"I'm going to tell," the Sixer said.

"You do what you have to," I said, pushing past

her to open the door. V was in her pj's, sitting on the cot, with her legs curled up against her. When she saw me, she motioned for me to sit down on the bed.

"I probably should stop trying to do you favors," she said, offering up a weak smile.

"Yeah, it doesn't seem to go so well."

"I'm sorry, Brit. I think I blew it. I didn't mean to. I thought everyone was gone, but Sheriff was there waiting for me."

"Missy tipped him off that I'd been snooping around. Besides, I got the files."

"You did? How?"

"It doesn't matter. I've got them."

"I won't be able to go through mine. Someone else will have to," V said, giving me a probing look. "Or maybe you already did."

"No, I haven't read it. That wouldn't be right. But I did see something in yours. By accident."

V let out a long sigh. Like a balloon losing its air. She slumped back against the wall.

"You're eighteen. Why are you still here?"

"Is that what you saw? My birthday?"

"Yeah. Why? What else is in that file? Whatever it is, does it explain why you're still here, why you of all people, you who hate this place so much, are still here?"

V shrugged and shrank farther back toward the wall. She was a tall girl, but she suddenly looked small, fragile, broken. I reached out to touch her wrist. She looked up at me, fear in her eyes.

"V, tell me."

She pinched the bridge of her nose and took another breath. "I lied to you. I lied to all of you. My dad's not a diplomat with the United Nations. Not anymore. He's dead." V started to cry.

I was stunned. All I could say was, "I'm so sorry."

She sat back, straightened out her shirt and wiped her eyes. "My dad *used* to work for the UN. We lived all over the place, in some pretty wild places: Ghana, Sri Lanka. His last assignment was in Baghdad, but Mom and I couldn't go with him that time; it was too dangerous."

"Oh God. He got killed in Iraq?"

V looked up at me through misty tears and let out a bitter laugh. "No. I mean that's what you'd expect to happen. I was at least a little prepared for that. Mom and I both were. People were getting blown up left and right. But no, he stayed safe there until the

UN cut his mission short. He came home and it was great. Mom and I were so relieved. Then two weeks after he got back, he and Mom drove up to Connecticut to see my grandparents. On the way home, their car was broadsided by a drunk driver. Mom walked away without a scratch, but Dad was killed on impact. Can you fucking believe it?"

I was numb. All I could do was stroke her hand and say, "Oh V," over and over. She kept going, the words tumbling out of her.

"After that, I kind of came unglued. Mom and I both did. It was more awful than anything I could've imagined. I missed him so much, and every morning for ages I'd wake up expecting him to be there. It was like losing him all over again. Every day. You know what that's like, don't you?"

I thought of my mom, the secret wish I'd nursed every morning that I'd find her downstairs, making breakfast. I nodded.

"So that was that. And then my whole world seemed to go berserk, and I felt like I couldn't trust my footing anymore. I just got scared to go out, scared I'd get hit by a car or electrocuted by a power line or bitten by a dog. It was totally irrational. It got so I couldn't even leave our apartment. It felt like doom was lurking in the most random of places. It was obvious that I needed some help. So here's the really crazy thing, Brit. *I'm* the one who chose Red Rock. *I* chose this place."

"Why? Why would you want to come *here*?"

"It felt safe to me. It still feels safe to me. We're way out here in the middle of nowhere. We're watched. We're taken care of. . . ."

"We're spied on. It's horrid. You hate it here. *You* hate it more than most."

V barked out a cutting laugh. "And I really *do* hate it. That's the oddest thing. I hate what it does to smart, mouthy girls like you. But for me, it's comforting. I know what to hate, what to fear, what to expect."

"And you also know how to keep yourself here."

"I guess. All the level demotions are just for show, although Clayton and Sheriff are as hard on me as anyone. My mom will let me stay here as long as I need to. She's petrified of losing me, too." V stopped and wiped her tears, her caustic laugh weakening to a nervous giggle. Then she looked up and bore into me with those eyes of hers. "Did you see your file?"

I nodded.

"And were there any bugaboos?"

"A letter from my mom, one that no one had shown me."

"Was she raving mad?"

"No, that was the strangest part. She was lucid. She knew what was happening to her. For that moment, anyway." I shook my head.

"What?" V asked.

"It's just that we'd like to think that craziness and sanity are on opposite ends of an ocean, but really they're more like neighboring islands."

V stared at me. "Is that what scares you? The thought that Brit Hemphill may be living a little too close to the island of the crazies?"

"Everyone else seems to think I'm already living on Crazy Island."

"Like who?"

"Clayton. Dad. I never told anyone this, but he came to visit me in the spring, and while he didn't admit as much, I could tell that's what he thought."

"Forget your dad. What do *you* think?"

I felt my shoulders retreat into a defensive shrug, but then I pulled them back down. V had come clean to me, and it was my turn. I owed it to both of us. "I'm scared," I said, my voice a tiny croak.

"Of what?"

"That I'm going to end up like her, that it's my destiny," I whispered.

"And what makes you think it is?"

"I look like her, I sound like her, I act like her, like she did when she was younger."

"But I thought your mom was the coolest, that everyone loved her."

"She was," I said.

"Then you should be thrilled to be just like her."

"Not if the end of that path is insanity," I said. And then it was all out there. Everything. It was said out loud. V didn't stroke my hand or say my name or hug me. She just watched me, her eyes sharp and glinting and wise.

"Cinders, I would've thought you of all people would know better. There are no wicked stepmothers and there are no fairy godmothers, and there are no Prince Charmings. There is no preordained destiny. *You* get to decide that. You decide your destiny."

"But what if I have it? Like a sickness. Inside me."

"Then you have it, and maybe one day it gets you.

But you decide how you live your life in the meantime. You can hide in fear. Or you can live life."

I looked into V's eyes. She was sitting up straight again, the fragile little girl gone for now. She was my tough-ass friend, my sister. And she was right, in more ways than one. "Maybe it's time you took your own advice," I told her.

Her gaze found mine and held it for a second. "Maybe you're right."

Chapter 26

If Bebe and Cassie thought I was foolish to attempt it, Ansley and Beth thought I was downright nuts. When I called them with my plan, they were dead against it. I told them it was the only way.

I didn't have a chance to tell V what I was going to do, but I thought she'd approve. Her words, after all, were driving me.

I broke out the same way I had in March, through the same unarmed door, jammed open with a rock. And Ansley and Beth were waiting for me the same as before, only this time with more trepidation than anticipation.

"Are you sure this is a good idea?" Ansley asked. "You don't exactly have a good track record."

"*We* could bring him your files," Beth suggested.

"It's the only way. He's got this idea of us as these bratty, stupid kids. If I meet him in person, maybe he'll take me seriously."

"He might also blow a hole in you with a shotgun," Ansley said.

"Ans, don't scare her."

"Well, it's Utah. Everyone's got a gun, and he could mistake her for a prowler."

"I'm not a prowler. I'm a teenaged girl, and I don't get the feeling he spooks easily. He won't shoot me."

We drove on in silence, through St. George and up toward Zion, where what seemed like years ago I'd spent part of a night with Jed. Instead of cutting into the park, Ansley turned north until the road emptied out again. It was late, around 11:30, but when we pulled down the tree-lined drive to Henley's giant ranch, the lights on his three-story adobe house were blazing. At least I wouldn't wake him.

"We'll wait right here," Beth said.

"If he starts shooting, duck and run for the car," Ansley said.

As I walked up the front path, dogs started barking inside the house, and before I could ring the bell, the door opened. Henley was old, with a shock of white hair. He wore tattered old pajamas and held a fat book, his finger bookmarking his page.

"What the hell do you want this time of night?" he growled. "Don't tell me you're selling Girl Scout cookies."

I looked down at my Red Rock uniform. "Mr. Henley. My name is Brit Hemphill. I called you a few weeks ago."

"Not you again. I told you. I don't care." He tried to shut the door, but I shoved my foot into it. He turned around to look at me, kind of surprised, but he didn't close the door. I walked through it.

"I don't recall asking you in."

"I know, but just hear me out. Here." I presented him the file the Sisters and I had amassed. It was almost as thick as his book.

"What's this?"

"Evidence. About Red Rock Academy."

Henley guffawed. "Evidence? What, that they're using dog meat in the tacos?"

"I know it seems funny to you, but I can assure

you, there are some serious transgressions going on at the school. And yet no one seems to care. No one believes us."

"I've heard about your school. It's for rich little drug addicts and runaways," he said, eyeing the tattoo on my arm. "I've no interest in that."

"Please, if you would just read this. Take a look. Evaluate it."

Henley picked up the file, gave the folder a cursory glance and handed it back to me. "Stop wasting my time, kid. It's past your bedtime, no more games." He started to walk toward the kitchen.

"Why won't you just look at it?" I shouted. "Why won't you give us a chance?"

"I gave you a chance last time by not calling your bloody principal. And I'm giving you a chance now. A chance to leave before I call the police."

"Right, because authority is always right, Mr. Henley? Were they right in the Alabama town you grew up in, when they burned down black churches? Were they right when they bombed women and kids in Vietnam? Were they right when they locked up South African freedom fighters?"

He stared at me, his ears turning red. "You can't be comparing yourself to those people. You simply cannot."

"I'm not. I know it's not that bad. But it's still wrong. And no one seems to care about it because we're kids and our parents sent us to Red Rock. As if adults don't screw up, too!"

"Look, I feel your pain. But I'm not your man. Leave now."

"Wasn't it you who said that the only way to guard freedom was to question those in power? That's what you said when you won your first Pulitzer. Doesn't that hold true anymore? There's something happening in your backyard, and it's bad, and you're the only one who can help change it. We need someone to help us!" I was yelling now. "I read what you wrote. I know all about you. You used to care about injustice. Please, please listen to us."

I threw the folder on the floor, and before Skip Henley could call the cops on me, I turned around and ran.

• • •

"It's a miracle you didn't get caught," Cassie said. I'd cornered her, Bebe, and Laurel in the cafeteria the next morning.

"You are pretty lucky," Laurel said. "V's break-in still has everyone really nervous. I'm amazed you made it out. I'm amazed you came back."

"I know. Maybe I should've kept going. Then the whole thing wouldn't have been such a bust."

"Don't worry, Brit. I'm outa here in no time and I'll find someone who'll listen."

"Thanks, Cass. But all that evidence. Everything we risked our butts for. It's all gone."

"And you're sure he didn't bite?" Laurel asked.

"No way. You should've seen the way he looked at me. Like some dumb little girl. He thinks we're a bunch of spoiled brats, and what'd I do? I went and had a temper tantrum in front of him. Played right into that one. He thinks we're a joke."

"Don't beat yourself up," Cassie said. "You gave it your best shot."

"One day the tables will be turned, dears—all these old farts will be needing our help," Bebe said. "We'll let them rot while we get pedicures."

· · ·

A week after my field trip to Henley's, V pulled a little escape trip of her own, showing up in the quarry one afternoon and walking right up to us.

"Hey cowgirl, how'd you get sprung?" Cassie asked.

V looked at me and smiled. "I have my ways," she said.

"Always with the mystery, this one," Bebe said.

"Cassie's the *real* Houdini. What do you have, a month left?"

"Nah, three and a half weeks," Cassie said, her head bowed.

"Don't tell me," Bebe said, "you're sad to be going?"

"Not quite sad, but a dash mixed up. It's just, I'm goin' home." Cassie paused. I had never seen her look so defeated. "You gotta understand," she continued, "where I come from, they invented redneck there. And if you're so much as suspected of being different, it's like you're always in danger of getting found out, just waitin' for the 'Gotcha!'"

"That sounds like here," I said.

"Nah, it ain't the same. Here we're surrounded by so many people that don't fit in that we *all* fit in. Like when y'all met me." Cassie smiled. "None of y'all even flinched knowin' I might be gay. The punch line is that messin' with some girl got me sent here, to be fixed. And now that I'm here, my secret's out and I don't feel so alone."

"You willing to risk one final breakout?" I asked. "We want to send you off in style."

"Sure, why not? My parents have already booked my flight home, so there's no backpedaling now."

"There's supposed to be a big meteor shower in two nights. I thought we could sneak out, watch it. It might be a while before we'll all be together again."

"That sounds like a nice way to say farewell," Cassie said.

"Good, then it's settled. Two o'clock by the infirmary door. We won't go far. Just outside, away from the lights."

As we drifted apart, V called to me.

"I heard what you did," she said.

"Fat lot of good it did."

"Huge lot of good it did. You were seizing your destiny."

"Thanks. Are you seizing yours? Is that how you escaped Level Two?"

"I told Clayton that I was planning on checking myself out soon. Not right away. I need to work up to it. But I told her I'd walk out today if they didn't quit with the penal crap. And you know them, anything to keep collecting the cash. I'm on permanent Level Six until I leave."

"That's a step, I guess."

"That's all we can do, Brit. Take steps. Take enough of them and suddenly, you're somewhere."

Chapter 27

It was a beautiful night, the sky black as a patch of velvet, the stars like diamonds, with meteors exploding and fishtailing across the heavens. We sat out on a rock, me, V, Bebe, and Cassie. Although V began our meeting with a call to order of the Divinely Fabulous Ultra-exclusive Club of the Cuckoos, it didn't feel like that anymore. Maybe it was the air of finality. Martha was home. Cassie was leaving soon. V would be, too. There was no date yet, but it was going to happen. That night, V told the Sisters her secret. And I told them mine.

It wasn't over yet. Bebe and I were still stuck at Red Rock, still had to find a way out of the level gauntlet, but for one night at least, under a hail of flaming stars shooting across the galaxy zillions of miles away, none of that mattered. We weren't Sisters in Sanity. We were just sisters.

Chapter 28

There were two daydreams I used to nurse when things got really bleak. In the first, Jed was here. He'd come back to get me, to take me away. And in the second, the world finally wised up to Red Rock—and the powers of good came and shut it down.

Let me tell you, the powers of good, when they finally show, can look an awful lot like scary storm troopers.

"This is a raid. Girls, please get your clothes and leave the building. I repeat: Please take your belongings, go to the parking lot, and give your name to Agent Jenkins."

"Huh?" I rubbed my eyes. It wasn't light out yet,

wasn't time for roll call. What was going on? I sat up in my bed, and two guys with identical buzz cuts and mirrored glasses were in the doorway. I yanked my blankets around me.

"Please get dressed, take your personal effects, and move to the parking lot."

"Who are you?" I asked.

"FBI. This is a raid. No need to be frightened. You're all safe."

"What the . . . ?" Missy asked.

I hopped out of bed and looked out the window. There were twenty or more cars lined up, lights flashing. My heart started thumping.

"What's happening?" Missy asked. For the first time, she didn't act like my master. She looked scared.

"I don't know. I think they're raiding the school."

"Who is?"

"Federal agents."

"Why would they do that?" she asked tearfully. She looked so upset that for a second I felt bad. Only for a second.

I got dressed and scrambled outside. V, Cassie, and Laurel were already congregated in a circle, huddling against the early-morning chill.

"Did you know about this?" I asked V.

"I was just about to ask you the same thing."

Five minutes later, Bebe came bounding out, a huge grin on her face. "Oh my God, Brit. Did you make this happen?"

"I have no idea what's happening, let alone who made it happen."

We all just stood there and watched as 187 sleepy-eyed girls in matching Red Rock polo shirts filed out of the building. About fifty agents coated the place like ants on jam. After about an hour, a lady came around and checked all our names off on a list. "Please remain here. We will have breakfast coming for you shortly. Please do not leave the premises."

A while later, a truck showed up and a couple of agents went around distributing donuts, orange juice, and coffee. Coffee. It was like nectar, the taste of freedom. None of us knew what was going on, but to me coffee signified our return to the real world.

We kept asking what had happened, but no one would tell us much. Just that it was a raid. Red Rock was under investigation.

The morning wore on, and we stayed outside. We all sat in a big clump under the trees, drinking the bottles of water the agents had passed out to us. The lady with the clipboard came around again, telling us to stick around, that our parents had been notified, and those of us who were not picked up by nightfall would be bused into town until arrangements could be made.

"Oh my God, darling. We *are* getting out of here," Bebe gushed.

Cassie laughed. "Just my typical luck when I was a week shy of leavin' on my own steam. Still, I'm glad for y'all, for all us girls."

None of us could talk much. We just watched, riveted to the spectacle, unsure if it was really happening. Around lunchtime, parents started to arrive, hysterically racing to their kids, grabbing them in big hugs, like you always see parents do on the TV news after a school shooting.

It was Pam, whose dad lived in Vegas, who showed us the article. A three-page piece in the national newsweekly *American Times* magazine titled "Disturbing Behavior." Written by none other than veteran journalist Skip Henley. It was all in there and so much more: our stories, the insurance fraud, the stuff about Sheriff, quotes from former students, as well as commentary from psychiatrists on how ineffective and damaging Red Rock's brand of therapy could be. Bebe, V, and Cassie read over my shoulder.

After we'd finished, Cassie looked at me and whistled. "Well, would ya look at that?" she said.

"Darling," Bebe said. "I. Am. Speechless."

So was V. She just looked at me, her expression saying it all: *Did you do this? Did we do this? How did we do this?*

Only later would we find out the whole story, about how Martha's family had filed a complaint with their congresswoman, who had spearheaded a separate investigation. That investigation had been working toward a bust. That bust had been jumpstarted once Henley's article appeared. Sheriff was already being investigated for mail fraud. Only later would I hear that Henley had run after me, not to chase me out of his house, not to shoot me, but to slow me down so we could talk. When I'd beaten him to the truck, he'd gone back into his house, picked up the file, and gotten to work.

Only later would I find out what was to happen to my sisters: V, Bebe, Cassie, and Martha. Because at that exact moment, coming through the crowd was Dad.

He looked like hell warmed over—his eyes blood-shot, his skin pale, his hair greasy and unwashed. He held a twisted copy of *American Times* in his hand.

"Good article?" I joked, hoping to lighten the moment.

Dad didn't smile. He just shook his head. "I couldn't bear to read the whole thing," he said in a choked voice. "I couldn't bear to know what I'd done to you."

I felt a flash of anger, but unlike when he'd come in for his surprise visit, this time the anger was mixed with sympathy. "Don't you think it's time to stop doing that?" I asked.

Dad held his face in his hands. "Stop doing what, honey?" he asked wearily.

"Hiding from the truth."

He looked up at me and shook his head again, but his expression gave him away. It was that same mask of exhaustion, sadness, and fear he'd worn for a year straight as Mom had slipped away from us. Seeing Dad fall apart had always melted any anger I felt toward him, and looking at him so lost right now, part of me wanted to shield him from any more pain. But that wasn't doing either of us any favors. I took a deep breath and continued. "You're scared because you lost Mom, and you're scared that you'll lose me," I said. My voice started to break. "You're scared I'm going to end up crazy too. And that's why you sent me away."

Dad just kept shaking his head. "No, honey. I didn't send you away because of that. I sent you to the wrong place, but it was for the right reason."

"Don't you dare!" I cried. "Don't you dare lie to me. Don't you dare lie to yourself anymore. I love you and I always will, but I won't allow you to do this to us anymore. You sent me away because you think I'm damaged goods. Well, I'm not damaged goods. I'm her daughter. I'm Mom's daughter. And I loved her, and I lost her too."

Dad just stared at me. Then he pulled me into a hug. I could feel him shaking, and suddenly I was calm. It was weird because as he cried, my fear, anger, and sadness fell away. When Dad regained his composure, he held me at arm's length, looking at me as though he were meeting someone for the first time. He brushed a lock of hair out of my eyes and smiled. "When did my little girl become so wise?" he asked.

I laughed, feeling lighter than I had in years.

"Come on, there's some people I want you to meet," I said. I motioned toward the Sisters and was about to turn in their direction when I saw something—or someone—out of the corner of my eye. I did a double take. The sun was glaring down now, and my eyes were kind of misty, so I figured it was an optical illusion. Either that or my wishful brain playing tricks on me. Except then the optical illusion started talking too. It was calling my name. "Brit," it called. "Brit Hemphill."

"Jed." I tried to shout, but it came out a whisper.

Jed seemed to hear me anyway, because he was striding toward me now, his gaze focused on me like a laser beam. Dad, still holding my hand, looked at me and then at Jed. He seemed baffled for a second, and then his expression changed to one of recognition as he sized up the situation. For a moment, he looked worried and strained again, but I squeezed his hand and smiled at him, letting him know everything was going to be okay. That I was okay. Dad held on to my hand for a moment longer, squeezing back. And then he let go.

I ran to Jed, ran so fast that everything else seemed to blur around me. I flung myself into his arms and kissed him. Then I nuzzled my head into his neck as he planted kisses me all over my face. Behind me, I could hear the sounds of my Sisters cheering, applauding like it was the end of a really great movie. It was then that I understood that the ordeal of the last few years was finally over—and that something else was about to begin.

Five Months Later ...

Eight cities, eleven days, thirteen hundred miles, ten motel rooms, and twenty-seven Burrito Supremes later, I should have been ready to sleep for a month at the end of my first Clod tour, but in truth, I'd never felt more exhilarated. I loved playing live, and I was having a total blast test-driving my new songs—short, fast tracks with titles like "The Cinder Pile," and "Clayton's Soul Is a Black Hole"—not to mention spending every waking and sleeping hour with Jed. Being on the road made me feel like life's possibilities were endless. I felt free.

Which is kind of funny considering how recently I'd been anything but free. Part of me still can't believe I was allowed to go on tour. When I asked Dad if I could spend winter break on tour, I'd expected a knee-jerk no. But he listened, and then he admitted that his fears about my being in Clod were based on his own experience. He knows what lengths seventeen-year-old girls will go to just to *meet the band.* So I had to remind him that I'm not some groupie; I *am* the band.

A week later, Dad came to his first Clod show. Backstage afterward, I caught him staring at me—and not with his usual sad-scared look, either. In its place was this dreamy expression I recognized from times when I'd done something to make him proud. The next morning he told me I could go on tour— provided, among other things, I called him every day to check in. Our tour conversations were much better than our Red Rock calls were. Dad asked about the details of every show, and he even told me stories from when he was a roadie, a part of his life he hadn't mentioned in years.

Mom. Well, she's a different story. I went to see her and Grandma a few weeks after I left Red Rock, and she was, frankly, a mess. When she wasn't rambling on about radio signals being beamed in through her cavity fillings, she was staring into space. She didn't seem to know who I was, either. I paid her a second visit the day we played in Spokane. Jed insisted on coming along. Thankfully, there were no paranoid rants this time. Mom was sort of quiet and childlike; she smiled and even held my hand. After we left, part of me wanted to ask Jed if he was scared I might end up like my mom. But later at the show, I caught a glimpse of myself in the mirrored wall and finally realized that maybe the only way to answer that question was to stop asking it.

It probably sounds like a plot for some cinematic moment of musical closure, but the last stop on Clod's tour was Cafenomica, and not because of me. The cafe's booker had been after us for an encore ever since our gig in March. It was as if the entire under-twenty-five population of St. George came out to hear us play our second Cafenomica show. Beth and Ansley were there, jumping around like crazy. We rocked the place so hard that the windows vibrated.

The next day the rest of the band drove back to Oregon, and Ansley and Beth drove me out to Red Rock. I don't know why I wanted to see it again. For closure? To stare down my monsters once and for all?

But when I stood in what had been the quarry, with tumbleweeds and cinder blocks all around me, all I felt was . . . *over it*. The place held no power over me anymore.

I thought about the rest of the Sisters. It was like we'd all slain our dragons. Martha, now a healthy size 14, had taught her parents to accept her as is and was planning on competing in a plus-size beauty contest. Cassie started a gay-straight-bi alliance at her school (though she still claimed to be undecided on where she fell in that spectrum). And cynical, why-settle-for-a-boyfriend Bebe had fallen head over heels in love with some guy. at her new co-ed boarding school. Even V, who'd barricaded herself in a Utah hellhole just to feel safe, was planning on traveling around the world solo. V liked to joke that *we* were the brochure girls now. Except Red Rock hadn't helped us. *We'd* helped us.

Ansley and Beth dropped me at the bus station, where I caught a sputtering Greyhound to Grand Canyon Village. As I walked down the path toward our agreed-upon meeting point, I got lost in the view: layer upon layer of brown, red, and pink-hued cliffs leading down the gaping canyon to the jade ribbon of

the Colorado River. It beat anything I'd seen in pic-
tures, and I felt goose bumps tickle my arms. It was
then that I spotted them at one of the lookouts, sil-
houetted by the afternoon sun: Amazonian V, survey-
ing the grounds as if she owned the place. Stylish
Bebe, leaning up against the rail like she was on a
photo shoot. Smiling Cassie, pointing out something
down in the canyon. And wide-eyed Martha, camera
in hand, taking in all the sights. I paused for a second
to watch my Sisters there on the precipice. And then I
joined them.

Author's Note

Sisters in Sanity is a work of fiction. When I worked at *Seventeen* magazine, I wrote a story about behavior modification boot camps—places that were not quite as harsh as the fictionalized Red Rock Academy Brit attends, but that did share a lot of its more unfortunate characteristics. I met all sorts of teenagers who'd gone to these institutions. Some had been "escorted" from their homes in the middle of the night by strangers; others had been tricked into going by their well-meaning parents. I also talked to moms and dads who truly believed they were helping their children, although after hearing what had gone down at these boot camps—from their kids, from media reports, or from government investigations—some parents weren't so sure they'd made the best choice.

What made me so sad—and what made me want to write this book—was that many of the kids attending these schools obviously needed help. Some were into drugs, others were messing up at school, and still others had eating disorders or were battling depression. But the staff at these boot camps seemed intent on punishing their students, on breaking them down. What these teens really needed was to be built up. To be nurtured. To be understood. To be helped by qualified professionals. *That* is what therapy is all about.

There are times in life when it can really help to have someone to talk to. Most therapists care about their patients and want them to be happy and healthy. It's unfortunate that misguidedly hard-core "tough love" places like Red Rock still exist, but thankfully, they are the exception, not the rule.